Charlotte Whitney Eastman

The Evolution of Dodd's Sister

A tragedy of everyday life

Charlotte Whitney Eastman

The Evolution of Dodd's Sister
A tragedy of everyday life

ISBN/EAN: 9783337095352

Printed in Europe, USA, Canada, Australia, Japan

Cover: Foto ©Andreas Hilbeck / pixelio.de

More available books at **www.hansebooks.com**

THE
EVOLUTION OF DODD'S SISTER

A Tragedy

OF EVERYDAY LIFE.

BY
CHARLOTTE WHITNEY EASTMAN.

CHICAGO AND NEW YORK:
RAND, McNALLY & COMPANY.
MDCCCXCVII.

INTRODUCTION.

The boy, his surroundings and development, have been the subject of study to many thoughtful men.

Bishop Vincent in "Tom and His Teachers," Burdette in "The Rise and Fall of the Mustache," William Hawley Smith in "The Evolution of Dodd," and many others have presented studies on different phases of boy life.

But what of the sisters of these boys? Are they receiving as much thought and study as they require, or have they reached the Utopian age in their development wherein all things are so ordered as to evolve the best possible woman from the girls in our charge? It is very evident to any one giving the subject attention that we have not attained to that happy condition. There are many women who are variously failures.

For Dodd's sister I have chosen a type of woman who is become exceedingly common. She is the woman who has made possible those abominable discussions on the subject, "Is Marriage a Failure;" she considers that the divine purpose in her creation is the same as in the case of the lilies of the field; "They toil not, neither do they spin, yet . . . . Solomon in all his glory was not arrayed like one of these."

As a woman she is a failure, although society will not recognize her as such; for it never admits that a woman can be a failure in any but a moral sense.

To discuss her needs as they differ from the needs of the boy in the public schools has been the motive of this book. In undertaking this, it has been necessary to deal with some elements of school life that are rarely discussed, but without which the subject can never be truthfully dealt with.

The powerful influence of certain conditions in our schools upon the final character of this girl must become patent to any one giving the subject careful study.

But the school is not alone responsible for this failure. There is a combination of other forces that contribute to produce her. Some of these we find in the home; some in the moral conditions of our schools; and more than most people think in the physical development of our girls in the high school.

THE
EVOLUTION OF DODD'S SISTER.

BABYHOOD.

A new baby came last night at Dodd's house, and the boy had scarcely recovered from the fit of sulks into which he had gone on that occasion. He had been taken forcibly from his mother's warm bed by a strange woman and laid on the couch in the study. His vigorous kicks and screams soon brought his father, who found that it would require all his time and attention to quiet the young man.

He first tried to reason with him, but arguments were scorned. Then he tried the effect of his glass paper-weight, but it was dashed to the floor with a renewed volley of screams.

"Let papa sing to you," he persisted gently, but while music may have charms to soothe the savage breast, it utterly failed on this occasion.

"Would he like his papa to walk with him?" At the very suggestion he straightened out stiff and threatened to hold his breath.

"What would papa's boy like?"

Something certainly must be done to quiet this outrageous racket. It would annoy his mother.

"Would he like to play with the clock?"

Suddenly he paused in his screaming with a pose of his little body that might mean instant renewal if the clock were not quickly forthcoming. As a last resort the only thing in the whole house that his mother had persistently refused to let him have was brought down, and a few moments of peace were secured while Dodd did effective work among the wheels.

The father had a faint notion that his duty required him elsewhere, but Dodd continued to differ so emphatically upon that point that he was compelled to give his attention to the boy and the clock, and the more reluctantly he staid the more emphatic the boy was in his demands.

So the deluded father remained in the only place where he was of the least service, while the great tragedy in the next room was being enacted.

At last, much against its will, the little head fell on the father's shoulder, and Dodd was quiet.

With fear and trembling he laid him on the couch and tip-toed out of the room. As he stepped into the other room, the old doctor announced in an apologetic and sympathetic way,

"A daughter, sir."

The tone impressed the mother strangely; it came so far from expressing the thrill of pleasure that went tingling through her as she knew that a little girl had come to her heart and home. There was altogether lacking that note of triumph that this same doctor had given when he had announced the arrival of Dodd two years before. Of course she knew that second babies were not such congratulatory affairs as first ones; and if the first one was, as Dodd, not yet out of his babyhood, the doctor knew that the new baby had not come in answer to special prayers. That might have explained why the tone was sympathetic instead of congratulatory.

Not at all, dear mother. It would have been much worse if that had been the first baby. That is only a genteel way that men doctors have of telling you that you have not performed as praiseworthy an act in bringing a girl into the world as you did in bringing a boy.

In the coming century, when women have demonstrated that a man is as much out of place in presiding over a birth as he would be in caring for a new born babe, and women minister to women, the girl baby shall have a triumphant note all its own.

Women might just as well face the fact that, while the poets have in all time extolled them, legislators have expressed the real sentiment of men toward them, and doctors have ushered them into this world with a word of apology.

Now, there is a reason for this, that is as fundamental in humanity as the vertebral column. In the very earliest conditions of mankind they extolled above all other characteristics, brute strength. And to-day, in our boasted civilization, crowds will go frantic over a pugilist whose only attraction is his muscles.

In the very heart of our educational system, among the colleges of the land, the man who can jump or run beyond the ordinary will have his name trumpeted to the world, while his super-intellectual companion has only a small college circle for admirers.

There we find in humanity this love of physical force, and a corresponding contempt for physical weakness.

There was also a strong desire to oppress the weak. In those early times of our race the strong man was king and the weak man or the weak nation was scorned and oppressed.

O, civilized man, don't think for one moment that you are beyond it. In the laws of this country you will find abundant proof of the fact that whenever the interests of man and woman differ, the law favors the man. The same love of physical strength and abuse of physical weakness clings to us yet.

Only when women have used their intellectual force to oppose it have they ever been able to compel the law-makers to enact laws that will give them the same protection that it gives to the men. There has been a fatal mistake made if this old relation was to have been kept up. Fathers of the nation, drive the women out of the schools, or your great-grandsons will never be able to be the lords of creation.

Then there is another strong reason why this new girl baby called for sympathy. Away back in that early time when society was unformed, and the nations held their territory through their strength, every woman meant just so much more of a burden to the state; every man, so much more help; and naturally the advent of a boy was a cause of rejoicing.

No doubt the father strutted around as if he had done something to be proud of, and treated his friends to whatever in that day represented cigars and it may be beer.

What a pity it is that the roosters in the barn-yard can not know the sex of each egg that is laid! It would save them such an amount of crowing.

As society came more into form, the daughters were like other chattels; they must be disposed of to the best advantage.

The Catholic convent afforded a refuge for third and otherwise undesirable daughters. In fact, it has not been until a date within our memory that a daughter did not promise to be something of a burden to her father. And even now we find a good many fathers who consider that they have failed in their duty if they do not support their daughters in idleness, and daughters who remain long under these parental roofs soon acquire a feeling of pride in dependent womanhood.

But the modern girl who goes through college, and many others who come in touch with the spirit engendered there, have a growing feeling of independence, and a strong desire to be self-supporting.

We shall soon consider the daughter who sits in her father's parlor and waits for the conquering hero to come, as on a par with the man who consumes his time and energy in decorating himself and strutting about to be admired, and a feminine form for dude and dandy will be invented.

We have no current word to express feminine insipidity; not, as surely every observing person knows, because it does not exist, but just because there is a certain admiration for this kind of womanhood. The old oak-and-vine idea still prevails.

When this idea of something to be supported is eliminated from womanhood, the baby girl will be considered one of God's choicest blessings at her birth, even as she is now a few weeks later. It is strange how this feeling is confined to a short space of time after her birth.

Scientists tell us that the characteristics of our progenitors show themselves more plainly in our infancy than at any other time, and it is the same with this remnant of barbarism. The circumstances of the birth of the baby girl are no criterion of her future condition except in the heart of her mother. For let the world say what it will, the mother's heart is never satisfied until it has a daughter for its own. The home is made so lovely by her presence that the parents soon realize that nothing can ever take the place in the home that a little girl fills.

A profane old doctor once expressed the whole matter in a nutshell. He had been attending the advent of the third little girl, upon which occasion the father had ex-

2

pressed his disapprobation in very strong terms. With the freedom that only family doctors acquire he said,

"O, shut up. In a week you won't give a —— which it is."

And he was right. That third girl was her father's especial pride. A few years ago there appeared a series of articles in one of our magazines on the question, "Should the girl have a dowry?"

One writer said, "Now, why not say when the girl is born, 'We must now begin and save for Dorothy's dowry.'"

For the love of woman-kind, don't!

Just as she is hoping for a decent reception in this world, don't blast it all by saddling upon her parents a burden at her arrival. If Dorothy does not bring to her husband dowry enough in a helping heart and hand, let her go and earn her living in some other way. Not that a dowry is not a desirable thing, but train Dorothy to appreciate the fact that if she does her duty as wife and mother, she has earned her right to live, whether or not she ever brings a dollar into the family treasury.

Teach her, also, that the long hours of a mother's labor, although not so recognized in the laws of men, are just as valuable as a creative power as the day's labor of her husband; and though the law never recognizes her right to will a dollar of the family property away from her husband, that it is merely a man-made law, and she, before the bar of justice, is equal partner with him in all the rights of the family.

Teach her these things, and she will be of infinitely more value to the human race than a dozen dowries could make her.

But of these things the mother and father at the parsonage had little time to think.

The baby had come with that heritage of American babies, a weak stomach, and the whole list of patent foods were tried with little success, although each can came warranted to fit the case, adorned with the portraits of unnumbered fat and lusty babies that it had saved from an early grave. However, with much worrying from the mother, and with much complaint from the father as the dollars rolled out of his pocket, the baby survived through the first three critical months.

The little one was tended with all a mother's loving care.   It was not a baby that was scientifically trained in every respect. All the new ideas with regard to the care of a baby were not readily received by this mother.   To her many of them bore the stamp of masculinity, and did not appeal to her mother sense; and when a wise sister told her, "You should never rock your baby to sleep," her usual mildness was very much disturbed, and she showed more spirit than was consistent with the conventional minister's wife.

"I would like to know why I shouldn't rock my baby! Hasn't she cost me enough, that I shouldn't get every drop of sweetness out of her that I can?"

"Yes, but if you ever want to go away any place, you will always have to stay to rock the baby first. I think it a great nuisance. You might just as well train her to get along without you. She is a great deal better off, and you will have so much less care."

"Why, I enjoy these half hours with my baby better than I do going to anything."

"O, well, of course if you want to make a martyr of yourself, you ought to have the blessed privilege."

She did want to make a martyr of herself. The maternal love filled her whole being; and in the long years afterward, when she took the little worn shoes out of their corner in the old trunk, when the little feet that wore them were far along on their journey, and far away from the loving mother heart, as she pressed to her cheek the little empty shoes, how those moments all came back, when the little head lay on her shoulder, and the pink feet were crowded into the palm of her hand, and the velvet touch of the little fingers was on her cheek. The years of trouble and care that lay between faded away and she knew that never in the whole experience of motherhood were there sweeter moments than those twilight half hours when she rocked her baby asleep.

The little shoes that are stored away in the old trunk—what secrets do they hold that send the baby's memories crowding into the mother's heart faster and thicker than all the other little garments laid away? The little feet that wore them "must wander on through hopes and fears, must ache and bleed beneath their load," and the mother, who is now

"Nearer to the Wayside Inn,
   Where toil shall cease and rest begin,"

feels a wonderful rush of tenderness for the little feet that have left their impress on the little worn shoes.

———

"Well, this baby must have a name, papa."

"Certainly. Let us give her a good Christian name. My mother's name was Susannah. Suppose we call her Susan."

"Susan indeed! I'll never call this sweet little thing Susan. I think Berenice and Benita would be very pretty."

"Pure foolishness, both of them. Do let the child have a name with some character to it. I would like to give her one with some inspiration like Doddridge. Martha or Sarah would be a noble name."

"Why, if you must have a Bible name, let's take Ruth. That is pretty."

"Very well, if you like it. But don't give her a name that she'll be ashamed of if she grows to be a noble woman."

So Ruth she was called.

The chances were that Ruth would have discipline enough to bring out her nobility young, for Dodd's attitude toward the new baby could never be questioned. It was from the start

> "Muzzer's dot a baby,
> Ittle bitsy sing;
> Sink I most could put her

Froo my rubber ring.
Got all my nice kisses,
Got my place in bed;
Mean to take my drum stick
An crack her on the head."

And the moment that the mother's back was turned he proceeded to carry out his intention in some form or another, until she was willing that he should live most of the time in the street.

But the baby Ruth managed to live through it all in a marvelous way that only babies understand. She soon began to develop bewitching dimples, and to her mother's inexpressible delight, the little lock of yellow hair that hung on her fair white forehead curled into a ringlet, and the eyes, that were merely round and indistinct in their coloring, took on a most charming curve and shone with a soft violet light.

And the mother saw that her baby girl was beautiful, and she was glad. Dodd was not a beauty; but then, Dodd was a boy, and even her prosaic preacher husband could see the advantage of beauty in a girl!

She had heard him say only last Sunday in his sermon, when describing a man to whom this world had given all things good, that he had sons who were upright, noble, gifted in intellect and heart, and daughters who were beautiful.

Little difference though their hearts were small and cold and selfish, and their minds held no more than a sieve—they were beautiful.

Why should she not think it God's greatest gift to woman? Did she not see in her daily life—did not every poem and every story prove, that beauty is a great and wonderful possession? Had she not seen brilliant men and good men choose for their wives women whose only attraction, whose only endowment, was their beauty?

It was the exception when the judge left Maud Muller to her lot of raking hay. He usually married her in haste, and then when he contemplated the twins he "wished that

they looked less like the man that raked
the hay on Muller's farm."

And little Ruth was beautiful; no one
could question it. And, indeed, no one tried
to. On the contrary they vied with each
other in calling her a beautiful little darling,
and in presenting her mother with dainty
clothing for her to wear, so that when her
babyhood days were past and she was considered in the eyes of the law ready for the
moulding that the public school gives, little Miss Ruth, as she liked to be called, had
a very distinct and well defined idea of her
personal beauty and her pretty clothes.

GIRLHOOD.

That first day at school was an occasion that Ruth had looked forward to with eagerness, for she had plans for a small victory. The mild, adoring mother said with gentle persuasion, as she was being prepared,

"Ruth, dear, you ought not to wear your brown slippers. Auntie sent them to wear with your new dress. Your shoes will do very nicely for this fall at school."

"O, I don't want to wear those horrid shoes! Can't I wear them just to-day? I'll be just as careful. Auntie May won't care, I just know she won't, and I won't get a speck of dirt on them. Can't I, mamma?"

"I guess not, dear."

Down the round cheeks the tears rolled, for it was a matter of real grief to her.

"O, yes, please do, mamma; I want to

just to-day. I'll be so careful. I won't play at all."

"Well, if you want to so much, wear them. But I think you would have a much happier time if you wore your shoes."

The slippers were on in a twinkling, and, as the curls were being brushed, the next question was mooted.

"I'll want my new ribbons if I have those slippers, won't I, mamma?"

"They are so fresh that we must keep them for Sunday; the old ones are to be used for school."

"But this is the first day, mamma. I ought to have something different, you know."

"Well, only for to-day, remember."

"And my white apron that has the Swiss embroidery on it—I can wear that, can't I, mamma?"

"You will tear that if you try to play, my dear. The heavier one will do just as well."

"I'll be so careful; I won't play a single

speck. Aunty said those heavy ones looked so common, so she gave me this one just on purpose to look nice in. I'm sure she would want me to wear it."

"Then you must be very careful."

"O, I will."

Her first victory was won; for she felt that she would be the most "proud and stylish" girl that went to that school.

Her childish ideal was fixed, and she enlarged it as the years went by; but it was always the same ideal.

Fresh and sweet as a flower she looked as her mother gave her the last caressing pat and kissed her good-bye.

"Now you will be a good girl, I am sure, dear. You always are."

The sighs that had been inwardly heaved over unpromising brother Dodd when he made his first appearance in the school room were in strong contrast to the greeting that was accorded to this dainty bit of pink and white femininity, with eyes so moist and touchingly suggestive of the late grief over the brown slippers. The teacher came to meet her with manifest delight as soon as she saw her enter the door.

"O, you little darling! Have you come to school? Can you tell me what your name is? Where did you get those lovely curls and such cunning little slippers? You are going to come every day, aren't you? Won't you kiss me?"

O, yes, Ruth would kiss her, although herself not fond of promiscuous kissing. It would have been very improper to refuse to kiss the teacher; so she submitted in a very graceful way, and the young lady never discovered that it was other than a delight to the child.

With herself it was such a constant habit that she never imagined that there were natures to whom public and promiscuous kissing seemed excessively vulgar. She might have comprehended that in the light of hygiene it was dangerous, but that it might also be aesthetically offensive, never occurred to her.

These eternal kissers. If they would only confine their kisses to those whose tastes are similar to their own, they would not be such public nuisances. But no one escapes.

The teacher with the kissing habit has so many at her mercy. She ordinarily kisses only the attractive ones, but there have been reports of those with such ostrich-like stomachs that they could kiss the whole school. When they do what they are given to see is their duty in this heroic style, while it may be momentarily disagreeable to some, yet there are no aching or rebellious little hearts under the shabby aprons of little ones from lowly homes that wished they were pretty enough to be kissed.

The teacher was young and gushing. She was but lately a high school girl, and her apprenticeship in the training school had not given her the thoughtfulness for others' feelings that a few more years of life might give. She had a great deal of confidence in her own judgment, but her susceptibility to golden curls and pretty slippers was not diminished in the least.

Was it a part of that teacher's duty to cultivate vanity, and entirely ignore the feelings of little hearts that beat under plain gingham aprons? An admiring smile would have been just as dear to little Katie Kabrinski, indeed much dearer because of its rarity. But that young teacher was governed more particularly by impulse than principle in these matters, although, to be sure, it never occurred to her in that light. She had not learned to have much sympathy with plain folks. She belonged to a state, moreover, in which the legislators had failed to appreciate any advantage to be derived from the employment of more matured women as teachers.

Public schools are not philanthropic institutions to provide support for high school misses in preference to more experienced teachers, even though married. The woman, and especially the mother, of experience would have given plain little Katie one of those caressing words.

What if her hair was straw colored, with face to match, and the two little braided tails of hair were tied with shoestrings? Her heart was just as tender. The fact that there was no word for her gave her a most important lesson before the teacher had hung up the reading chart. She saw the value of beauty and pretty clothes, and learned at five what she would still believe at fifty, that beauty in a woman is, in practice, valued at more than the truest of hearts. The words "proud and stylish" were unknown to her, but she recognized their meaning, and was a ready devotee at their shrine.

Ruth had answered the teacher with dimpling smiles and a sweet "Yes, ma'am," and when the bell called the children together, the teacher looked for a seat for her. The only vacant one was found beside the little Russian girl.

She hesitated a moment and then said:

3

"Well, my dear, I guess you will have to sit here for the present." She did not say:

"I am sorry that such a sweet little darling must sit by that homely little thing in her Dutch blue apron and calf-skin shoes, but we will move you as soon as possible."

She did not say it, but each little girl understood it perfectly, and Ruth drew her apron very close to herself and tried by her manner of superiority to impress upon Katie that the difference between them was great. And Katie unhesitatingly believed her.

When the work of the morning began, and the teacher was trying to impress, first the script form—of course it was very important to have the script form first—and then the printed form of C A T, Ruth was comparing her finger nails with those of Katie.

Auntie May had often told her that she would be an aristocrat because her nails were so beautifully shaped, and she had resolved that she would never again play at making mud pies, for it just spoiled them. She saw that Katie's were short and square, and of course Katie could never be an aristocrat.

Katie's eyes were filled with admiration and interest, not for the picture cat, nor its script representative, but for the wonderful embroidery on Ruth's apron. This evident admiration entirely thawed out Ruth's intended hauteur, and she poked out one brown slipper and whispered:

"Auntie May gave them to me."

One after another she displayed the articles of her finery for Katie's admiration, and when each had elicited as much as it could, she drew up a corner of her dress just to show the edge of a dainty embroidered skirt to convince Katie that she was the same all the way through. When the lesson was finished these children had but a dim idea of it; not that they were dull, nor that the gushing girl teacher had not illustrated the subject to its fullest, but that the subject of clothes had so completely absorbed their attention that there was room for nothing else.

When Katie's admiration began to wane, Ruth drew herself together again with the sudden recollection that she had been too familiar. As soon as school was out, she found Beatrice, the banker's little daughter, and walked home with her. Katie was just behind them, but of course she could not walk with them, she was so common.

Ruth had really felt greatly attracted toward the admiring child, but Auntie May had told her mamma that Ruth ought not to be allowed to associate with common children if she expected her to grow up exclusive. Mamma had answered that she supposed she ought to be satisfied if her child grew up good. But to be sure, you could not help but expect something more from such a child.

So she knew that there were things expected of her, and she did not intend to ruin her prospects by walking with such a common companion as Katie Kabrinski.

On their way home Beatrice brought from her pocket a new shining five cent piece that had been given her if she would be a good child and not "fuss" about going to school. A paper bag of chocolate creams was soon bought, and this was a strong cement to the friendship thus formed.

"O, I just love chocolate creams; don't you?" was the way Ruth showed her appreciation.

"O, not very much; my papa brings me so many I'm most tired to death of them. We don't have hardly anything but candies and such things at our house."

"Neither do we," replied Ruth, spurred on not to be outdone by Beatrice in the matter of ennui as regarded all delicacies; "I have candy and nuts and oranges and such things almost every day. O, we have pie, too; I think pie is just splendid, don't you?"

"O, some kinds. If it's mince with lots of raisins or lemon pie with frosting. I won't eat any other kind. I tell you, I'm just mad if mamma has any other kind."

"So am I. I always have two pieces."

Now, Beatrice did not state the exact truth in this conversation, but Ruth came much farther from it, for the parsonage pocket-book did not afford pie and candy on all occasions. But Ruth would have been been greatly mortified if Beatrice had known the exact truth in regard to that matter.

Beatrice did not have tapering fingers and almond shaped nails like hers, but her father was the richest man in the town, and she had grown-up sisters who had lovely dresses and drove in an elegant carriage and went to dances, and Ruth thought that probably they had all the chocolate creams that they could eat. From her lips Beatrice should never get a confession that chocolate creams were a rarity at the parsonage.

By the time the little stomach was well under headway doing its duty for the creams, her appetite for the mashed potatoes and beef steak that her mother set before her for her dinner was anything but keen, and she waited in pouting silence for the dessert.

Rice pudding, and not a single raisin in it! However, the cream and sugar were some inducement, and she ate her share.

"Why, Ruth, aren't you going to eat anything but pudding for your dinner?" asked anxious mamma.

"O, I don't care for such plain food." And Ruth thought she was growing really aristocratic.

Beatrice with her five cents was now Ruth's constant companion from school. The little bag of candy was regularly consumed, and the mother wondered why Ruth had so little appetite for her dinner, and seemed not to sleep well. Finally she grew peevish and her breath was fetid, and the mother was sure that she had worms.

They kept her home from school for three days and fed her on turpentine and sugar; then she was very much better.

There really was nothing like turpentine for worms!

But Ruth was afraid that some one would get her seat beside Beatrice—for as soon as possible the teacher had changed her seat from the one beside Katie—and she wanted to get back to school. She had apparently forgotten now that she had ever known Katie, and was careful not to give her so much as a glance of recognition if she passed.

Auntie May had told her that she must be exclusive, and of course that meant that she must not speak to any one who was not aristocratic. She and Beatrice were the most aristocratic girls in school, and the teacher knew it; for did she not treat them differently from the other girls?

If they did not know, when asked, what she had been drilling the children on, perhaps for days, she very carefully went over the work again. If there were any small favors or privileges they always got the lion's share. They told each other that they had the privilege of passing the drawing books and being monitor on the stairs oftener than any one else. The teacher generally asked them for the answers to the easiest questions and gave them the easiest words to spell.

Some of the hateful, jealous girls said that they were pets. Of course they were! Why shouldn't they be?

Before the first year was done they came to expect special consideration as a matter of course, and to skim over the hard places. Application was a process that their little intellects knew nothing about, for their education was conducted on the plan of throwing facts at them until they stuck, or until a part of them stuck. Ruth sat through that whole first year, a target for the little homeopathic pellets of human knowledge that the teacher persistently threw at her.

Now, it takes no intellectual force to make a target of one's self in this way, and when the fact that c-a-t spells cat had been repeated often enough the child's intellect comprehended it. Not as a built-up thing, made of parts that she could take apart and put together again in other forms and with other sounds, but as a thing that she grasped as a whole, and which it required no more intellect to comprehend than a parrot would need to learn items much less simple.

At the end of nine months of school confinement she could tell you all the words in a small primer—words that had been persistently thrown at her in the same way.

Then there was that beautiful chart in number work. That teacher had spent hours in pasting on card-board first one apple, trying to get into those young and undeveloped minds the idea of "one thing." It was one large, red, luscious apple, such as would make the mouths of any young animal water with desire for it.

The beauty and lusciousness of it would help to transfer the idea of what "one thing" alone and unassisted might look like.

.When the conscience of the teacher was satisfied that every child in the room could fully comprehend and appreciate the fact of "one thing," she turned a leaf and disclosed two objects. Now there were two groups of two objects—two girls and two plums, and the drill began in earnest.

"If one plum is taken from two plums, how many plums will remain? If one girl and one girl stand together, how many girls will there be? If two plums are divided between two little girls, how many plums will each little girl have?"

That teacher would not have allowed one of those children to use the fingers; that was tabooed from the childish study of arithmetic long ago; but she substituted the plums and dolls for the fingers and imagined that she was using a method far different from the old-fashioned one.

The object in view when the departure from the use of the fingers was first made was to force the child, as soon as possible, into abstract thinking, but the abuse of the object work substituted has made the conditions in teaching number work very similar to those before the reform.

Now Ruth could have told her teacher very quickly that if mamma gave her two pennies, and papa gave her two pennies, she would have four pennies. Moreover she could have told her that it would take one more penny, that she had coaxed brother Dodd for in vain, to make enough pennies to buy a bag of peanuts.

She had not learned at that time that peanuts were vulgar. At ten she would insist that she had never tasted a peanut.

Ruth had not been "born long" on figures, yet her mother could have told you that while she still lisped in baby notes she knew two objects when she saw them.

O, deluded school teachers, do you think a child knows nothing when it comes to you? Ask any fond mother that question and you will soon find out about it.

For three months the young woman hung that chart before those little human beings, and with a hundred times the persistency of Mr. Smith's rat trainer she tried to impress upon them what the component parts of four were—a thing they already knew.

The rat trainer could teach a common rat to fire a cannon or walk a rope in two weeks, yet these little intelligent beings could not learn the component parts of numbers under ten under three months.

What difference did it make that they well knew how many pennies in a nickel? That would not help the teacher out when the superintendent came in to inspect results. Now she could call on that pretty little Ruth, and have her say in her sweetest tones,

"Two dollies and two dollies will make four dollies."

She must have something to make a definite showing with, and so term after term these little ones are drilled and drilled until their knowledge is all done up in little packages, labeled and pigeon-holed so as to be produced on demand.

It was by this kind of work that the ability of Ruth's teacher was to be judged. Her retention or promotion would depend probably to a great extent on what the superintendent said of her work, and her first object must be to drill the class so as to make a ready and attractive display of what the children knew.

When our interests are dependent on doing work in a certain manner, it takes the spirit of a martyr to sacrifice outward success to inward convictions.

Ruth's teacher was not troubled in soul with inward convictions. She was content to rest upon the superiority of those above her in authority, and felt no responsibility for any method whatsoever that she was expected to use. They were given to her ready-made, and she put them on like any other garment, or used them as she would text books.

Were the little intellects under her care developing? Were they being used in the daily school room work? She did not know.

She did not care a great deal. Much less did she care what those same little minds were doing on the play-ground.

Certain it was that they were constantly receiving more food for thought than under the teacher's direction where they worked for weeks at what most of them could have learned in a vastly shorter time.

To make the child think consciously was the very last result contemplated. Ruth was capable of thinking. She could go through a regular logical process when she was managing her small affairs at home; but when she came to school nothing was expected of her, not even to remember. She was simply drilled until she could not help remembering.

Any pedagogue imbued with the idea of the wonders of our new education would tell you that she was infinitely more fortunate than her grandmother, who learned her letters at the end of her mother's knitting needle, and was expected to learn by herself all that she possibly could.

Far from it. Whatever the other faults of her education, that grandmother was compelled to think according to her capacity.

What a boon it would have been to Ruth, with her delicate, modern stomach and her sensitive American nerves, to have reveled in fresh air and sunshine for a large part of her time, as the A, B, C scholars of her grandmother's time did, instead of sitting under this constant fire of facts.

Those were the days when that grandmother was laying up a store of nerve and muscle for the days of her necessity.

Every romp through the woods; every breath of pure air that she drew as she filled her apron with dandelions or scaled the lichens from the old fence rails; every ray of sunshine that browned her cheek and sprinkled freckles on her nose, were strengthening the fibre of her small body, and would in the days of her womanhood be of infinitely more value to her than all the drill of that primary room.

But Ruth appeared to enjoy the school work.

O, yes, she adored the young teacher who dressed so prettily and entertained them so nicely in the intermissions between the seasons of drilling.

But that is no criterion as to the usefulness of a teacher. The teacher most popular with the pupils is quite as often as otherwise the teacher who has the least power to make them think. Because she can succeed in making them obtain facts without any conscious effort on their part, she is a delightful being to the child; but it no more represents development than teaching a parrot the same thing.

But Ruth's mother would never have believed that the teacher who could so attract Ruth to school was anything but perfect.

What a delight to see Ruth start to school each morning eagerly, with smiling face.

What a contrast to the judge's daughter, whose mother thought she was so much more competent than the trained teacher,

4

who called her little daughter to come to her room each morning for her lessons. What flouts and pouts and rebellion, as much as were allowable, were heard and seen.

But that same firm "You must" was repeated each morning until the child submitted to the inevitable, not because she loved it, but because a higher power willed it.

"Spare the rod and spoil the child" sounds very harsh to modern ears, but there is a germ of truth in it that will endure while childhood lasts.

How was it at the end of the first year with the judge's daughter and the minister's daughter?

The school girl could read. anything in her primer at sight; beyond that primer she knew not one word.

The mother-taught child read with avidity from a hundred books of childish interest.

Was there then such a difference in the

children? Not at all. One was taught to think; the other was taught to repeat.

The alphabet and multiplication tables may be the foundations of all knowledge, but capacity for thinking is the foundation of all wisdom.

But if the children were not compelled to think during school hours, certain it is that at the times when they were free to associate with the children of all grades their minds were much more active, their lessons more graphic, and their impressions far more lasting.

What fun it was to sit on the front steps munching their candies and watching those common girls romping.

There was a great deal of whispering and giggling as Beatrice would point to some faded dress and say,

"Isn't that a beauty! I would like to wear it to the club dance."

"O, yes, I would like to be married in it."

"And have your hair tied with a shoe-string."

"O, yes, and blue stockings."

"O, dear, O, dear!"

They would have to stifle their paroxysms of laughter in their handkerchiefs.

Then the high school girls would come down and talk to them. These girls had gone through many of the same experiences that were in prospect for these children, but they belonged to families where money was not abundant enough to provide the clothes necessary to take the position in school life their desires dictated. They looked upon beauty and wealth as the only really desirable things in life, and they showed these two children, by their constant attention and admiration, that they considered them superior to the common children.

Whenever they met them they had to say,

"O, Ruth; what lovely curls," or "What a stunning complexion you have," or

"Say, Beatrice, do your sisters belong to the Two-Step Club?"

"Of course they do," Beatrice would say.

"Do they walk, or do their fellows come to take them in a carriage?"

Beatrice was not at all sure, but she did not allow that to influence her much.

"Why, in a carriage, of course."

"Well, say, Beatrice, do their fellows come to see them in the morning or in the evening?"

She was not quite clear which ought to be the proper time; so she tossed her head and said:

"The idea!"

So the girls continued to quiz her in regard to the lives of those sisters until she was observant of all their movements, and kept herself as well informed as possible, so as to excite the admiration and envy of these school girls.

To Ruth the life of these elder sisters was fairy land. She began to feel a scorn for the simple life at the parsonage, and determined to go and live with Auntie May just as soon as she was old enough.

Ruth and Beatrice did not spend their time on the play-ground in romping games. Ruth was afraid of spoiling her clothes or her complexion, and Beatrice very much preferred the talks on the stairway, or in the groups and knots of the larger girls, where such conversations were the common thing.

"I saw Mrs. S—— out riding yesterday and she had a lovely dress with a parasol to match. She don't have any young ones hanging around her."

"Well, I guess she don't. She's too smart for that."

"Just look at Mamie T——. She's had two since she has been married, and she can't go to a dance or anywhere else."

"Well, she never did know anything. I tell you, if her father hadn't had the stuff, he'd never have married her."

Then there were giggles and whispered sentences. When Ruth and Beatrice wanted to know what was said, they were made

to give solemn promises "never to tell," and
the whispered sentences were passed on.
There was a shout of amusement at the puz-
zled look that came into the young faces,
and explanations were given that called
forth wondering "Oh, my's" from the children. But these were given only after repeated promises "never to tell their
mothers." In this way it was that there
came to those children their first knowledge
of the most vital principle in human existence, accompanied by suggestions that were
vulgar and coarse. Their very first impressions, that should have been as delicate as a
mother could make them, and that should
have been presented to them free from any
associations that would tend to vitiate their
sentiments, were rendered distorted and untrue.

When Beatrice's sister gave her the beautiful little poem to read beginning,

"Have you heard of the valley of BABY LAND,
The realm where the dear little darlings stay;
Till the kind storks go, as all men know,
And O, so tenderly bear them away?"

she brought it over for Ruth to read; and they giggled for a whole hour over it.

It was about this time that a little new comer was expected at the parsonage, and the mother remarked to the father one day, "I dread Ruth's questions when the baby comes. She was troublesome enough last time, and she is two years older now. I can't bear to tell her an untruth, and she is so young I hate to spoil her beautiful illusions."

"Oh, don't worry over that. Such matters regulate themselves," the father answered, and he felt that he had said a very wise thing.

"Yes, I suppose they do. I know that she is a peculiarly pure minded child. I never knew her to say a naughty word but once, and that was almost two years ago. I reproved her very severely, and told her never to say such a thing to any one again, and I never knew her to repeat it or say anything like it."

"That is the right way. Just nip such

things in the bud and they will come out all right."

But Ruth's mother was not annoyed with a single question. The baby was no surprise to her. She expected it the night that her mother suggested that she go over and stay with Beatrice.

Beatrice had told her many times that it was a shame that they had to have so many babies at their house just because they were minister's folks. Just as likely as not she would have to stay in and rock the baby now instead of going walking after school.

Ruth felt that this was all true and that it was an imposition on her. She walked into the house in the morning with conscious dignity, prepared to show her disapproval of the whole affair if her fears should be realized.

When she came in her father said:

"Ruth, God sent you another brother last night. Don't you want to come in and see him?"

"I don't care to," Ruth answered, very stiffly, and went to hang up her wraps.

Realizing that such conduct would hurt her mother the father said: "You had better go in and see him and speak to mamma. She will want to know that you have come."

Ruth walked in very grandly, and without deigning to notice the little white bundle, said:

"I have come back, mamma."

"Yes, dear. Did you know you had a new brother? Here he is. Isn't he sweet?"

Ruth did not answer. She asked no questions, and showed no surprise.

Her mother was astonished, and thought her a remarkably sweet child. She had never heard her speak on any of the subjects that are usually tabooed between mother and child, and for that reason she supposed the child had no thoughts on those subjects. She had congratulated herself at the last W. C. T. U. meeting, when the woman sent by the Union was discoursing on the subject of social purity, and in the course of her remarks said:

"If women would recognize this element in their girls as well as in their boys, we could work so much more intelligently."

In her girl she would have nothing of the kind to deal with. Of course when the proper age should come she would impress it upon her that elements of that nature were extremely degrading. At present it was entirely unnecessary to be concerned about the matter at all, for she was sure that Ruth had never had her attention called to any such matters, for the child never spoke of them. The mother never dreamed that long before, when she had sharply told Ruth never to mention the subject again to any one, she had sealed the child's mouth to her, and kept her from the very source from which her information should have come.

It is a mistaken idea that a mother knows her child better than any one else. She does not, unless she has that exceedingly rare faculty of being able to govern and at the same time to keep the child's heart open to her.

The fear of censure, the dread of long drawn sermons, have kept many children from telling the mother the very things which they have the most need of knowing.

Ruth's mother considered it her duty to correct her children's wrong-doing by long, grave sermons that were referred to after the misdemeanor, until she thought the child was properly impressed.

Very early in her association with Beatrice, Ruth had learned that discretion in these matters was far more comfortable than open confidence.

With considerable interest she had asked her father if he knew that Johnny Jones' father was a miser.

"Who says he is a miser?"

"Oh, Beatrice; and she told him so today."

"Told him so? Why did she do that?"

"Oh, 'cause he stuck his foot in her tri-
cycle."

"Were you with her?" Ruth's mother
asked her.

"Yes, ma'am."

"What did you say?"

"Oh, I didn't say anything. I only stuck
my tongue out at him." The rebuke that
followed this confession was as severe as
if to stick out one's tongue were the first
step in a career of vice, and Ruth drew between herself and her parents another
screen. It was this undue severity in small
offenses that satisfied the mother that she
was doing her whole duty by her children,
while graver things went by unnoticed.

In the hot-house of the public schools,
where her knowledge was being forced in
many ways beyond her childish years,
where the sweetness and innocency of her
very tender age were being colored and distorted by contact with ideas and feelings far
beyond her, she needed the closest contact
with a wise mother heart.

But the mother was entirely ignorant of these conditions, and one of the first lessons that Ruth learned was to conceal from her the very things in which she most needed her advice.

Mothers have been trained for generations to consider any interest in the greatest question in nature on the part of the woman as indicative of the woman's eternal disgrace.

If this is seen in a girl, they say that it signifies a low nature, and it is one of the hardest things to make a mother believe. If they see it in a son, they are grieved, to be sure, but comfort themselves with the thought that it is very much like boys. No matter how low or foolish a thing a boy may do, he hears that "it is just like a boy," and he is very soon convinced that nothing much is expected of him in this regard.

It is this difference in the ideal that is set before the girl and the boy during their years of development that is one of the most potent factors in their final difference of moral perception. Occasionally there has been a mother wise enough to withhold her rebuke or instruction until some other time than the moment of confidence, and has discovered startling facts of what her little girl has been learning at school.

She has been able perhaps by careful explanations, by revealing as much of the truth as she has deemed wise, to instruct her child in such a manner that the pernicious influence of contact with the minds that interpret nature basely has failed to make any lasting impression. Most mothers, like most teachers, are blind, deaf and dumb to the verbal commerce of the recess.

Ignorance on the part of the mother, a lack of a right feeling of responsibility (together with a foolish modesty) on the part of the teacher was gradually deforming the moral constitution of this child.

She had now reached an age beyond childish things. Her companions were no longer playmates. They were classed together as distinctly as were the young men

and women ten years their seniors. Ruth
and Beatrice had a clique of their own, and
any other little girl not considered worthy
of their recognition they could cut with all
the hauteur of a hardened society dame.

They measured a girl by her clothes, by
her artificial airs, by the way she curled
her hair, by her style and by her desire to
have "regular company." Her grandmother and vulgar little girls might talk about
beaux, but that was very far below them.
They had "regular company."

Ruth's curls were patted and petted with
as much solicitude as they would have received from the most aspiring young society
lady.

It was at this time that Ruth's father
moved into the country. When it was announced at the supper table that the next
year the family would spend with Grandpa
Stebbin, the tears came to Ruth's eyes, and
her heart sunk with as great a sense of
misery as it did in after years over greater
sorrows.

"Why, just think, Ruth, you can have all
the golden-rod that you can wear now. I
wouldn't feel so badly. Mamma remembers
such delightful times when she was a little
girl on the farm. You can't have Beatrice,
of course, but cousin Katie is there. She is
a sweet little girl."

But it was all in vain. She went from
the table to her own little room and cried
until there were no tears left, and only
broken sobs told of her grief.

She could not have told that wild flowers
were only dear to her when she wore them
in the belt of her white dress, and people
stopped her to say:

"Well, I don't know which is prettiest, the
flowers or the sweet little face."

The fresh air was more liable to spoil her
complexion than to do anything else, and
as for cousin Katie, she knew she would
be a horrid, pokey, countrified thing.

What were woods, if her set couldn't have
a picnic in them? Or a coasting hill with a

lot of country boys that never knew how to be nice to a girl?

And the sobs would begin again.

She did not go to see Beatrice for several days, and then she suffered agonies of mortification to have to tell her that they were going to live in the country.

Beatrice poured out all the sympathy that she could command, and finally suggested that she write to Auntie May, and see if she could not help her.

The childish letter of woe brought a ready response, and Mr. Weaver's sister again urged that Ruth be allowed to come and stay with her, through the winter at least.

Consent was finally given to this, and Ruth, radiant with joy, left for her winter home in the city.

.In the school in the city she found a class, or "set," as she called it, that corresponded with the one to which she had belonged. Their clothes were more elaborate, they had more money to spend, but their conversation and moral influence were just as

pernicious as were those in the smaller
school.

She spent only three months here before
the holidays, and returned to pass that week
with her parents.

Only three months; but in that time her
fond auntie with solicitous care had kept
her mind on dress and fashionable amusements, and had rendered her more than ever
devoted to the artificial life that she had begun so early.

In the country she found it hard to be
polite to the people she met. The Christmas tree and the simple Christmas pleasures filled her small soul with disgust; and
when one of the assistants called out "Ruth
Weaver," and brought her from the tree a
little doll dressed by her grandmother's loving hands, she thought it "perfectly dreadful," and was so glad that none of the girls
could know anything about it.

She looked with disgust at cousin Katie,
showing its twin sister with evident pride to
her companions. What would Beatrice

think of it? And she thought of last Christmas morning when she had seen Beatrice turning up her nose in scorn at the handsome doll that had been given her.

"Just as if she were a baby!" she said.

At home she did not attempt to conceal from her grandmother the fact that she was far above dolls.

"I thought you had no doll and that maybe you would like one if you had it. Katie liked hers, didn't she?"

"Oh, yes, of course," said Ruth indifferently. Then with fine scorn she said:

"And papa, do you know that some of those children really thought that Santa Claus put those things on the tree for them? How ridiculous!"

"It's a very foolish thing," her father answered, "to put such notions into children's heads. I should like to have been there and told the exact truth to those children. I wonder that parents do not realize the harm that they do to children in filling their heads with such nonsense."

"What harm do they do, William?" the grandmother asked.

"What harm? Why, mother, I am astonished that you ask such a question. They tell an untruth to their children, and not only do the harm that an untruth always does, but they shatter the children's confidence in their veracity. When a child discovers that its parents have told a falsehood, it can never have the same confidence in them as before. And then there is absolutely no use in it. It certainly does the child no good."

"Why, I think it does a great deal of good. It helps to make Christmas enjoyable for one thing. I found out a long time ago that of all the theories that I started out with for raising my family, there is only one that has stood the wear and tear, and that is let the children have all the good times they can. As to making them think that we were not to be depended upon,— Mary, how was that? Did you ever lay that up against me?"

"Well, no, mother, I don't think that we did. I'm very sure that we children always depended upon your word and father's as though it were law. The little German children always believe in Santa Claus."

"Oh, well, the Germans are a myth-loving people; very different from us Americans."

Grandma Stebbins knew nothing about myth-loving, but she did know that every child that is robbed of its Santa Claus has lost something of real value.

Why should we sacrifice even the pleasures of our little ones to this craze for the realistic?

The winter went by, the beautiful spring was come again, and Ruth was sent for to spend the remaining time of her father's vacation in the country.

Auntie May consoled her in every way she could, and at last promised her that if she would not feel too bad she would send her a piano just as soon as her hands were large enough to reach an octave.

It was a great trial to leave her beautiful home. She felt that she belonged there; that she had been created for just such a life, and that to have to go into the "horrid country" was an imposition.

When she found herself sitting beside her little trunk in the small room at Grandpa Stebbins', she opened it and looked at each memento of her school friends with an air of melancholy that might have been bestowed upon a long lost sister.

There was the half of a ten cent piece that she and Beatrice had divided as pledges of their eternal friendship. There was a hickory nut with a face carved on one side, a memento of their last picnic. There were some dried roses that had been thrown to her at the last school exhibition. There were these and a score of other little treasures.

She looked them all over caressingly, and the sobs came very thick as she looked out of her window down the dusty lonesome road. Her grandmother called her at the stairway:

"The turkeys are coming home, Ruth. Don't you want to go out with baby and me to see them?"

Ruth went down, not that turkeys had any attraction, but that it was insufferable to remain where she was any longer.

"Yes, dear," the mother said, "you will like to see the turkeys. Mamma always used to watch for them to come home when she was a little girl."

She met her grandfather in the yard.

"What! Crying, little one? Oh, that will never do. You'll spoil those pretty blue eyes. Those were only meant to smile with." That was the first drop of healing on her wounded heart, and it brought the faint ghost of a smile.

But the turkeys and cows and young lambs and even the playful kittens were of no avail. She had no heart for anything of the kind. She gathered her dress around her, and was in constant fear that it might get soiled.

The children started off to school the next morning. The grandfather took them over in the big wagon, "until Ruth should get used to the walk."

"Now you won't be lonesome any more," he said as he unloaded them at the gate. "Here's your little cousin, Katie. She's just the nicest kind of a little girl. Now go get acquainted as fast as you can. She'll soon loosen your little tongue and you'll be the best kind of friends in ten minutes."

Katie stood bashful and smiling, with a heart full of welcome and kindness for this little city cousin.

But for Ruth one glance was enough. Be friends in ten minutes, indeed! As if she could ever be friends with a girl who had her hair combed straight back from her forehead, and a gingham apron on, and great heavy shoes! She did not dare to "cut" her as she wanted to, but Katie understood very distinctly at the first glance that she was regarded as an inferior being.

"Now take her up to the school, Katie, and let her get acquainted with the teacher and the other girls. Be good to her, for she is a little bit home-sick you know."

Home-sick! It was a magic word. Katie had been home-sick once when her mother had left her for a whole week, and she knew the full meaning of that dreadful malady. So it was with a heart full of sympathy that she walked with Ruth up to the school house, and in her simple, child-like way, told the teacher who she was. Ruth wrote to Beatrice that that introduction was just killing. When the children were seated, Ruth had an opportunity to study the teacher in her accustomed analytic way. The result was certainly shocking to her.

She wrote to Beatrice that the teacher was a regular Irish girl, and her face was full of freckles, and she knew that her complexion had never had a bit of care, and O, dear! she wished she could see her waist.

Well she just knew she didn't have any corset on at all, and her skirt had three ruffles on,—just to think! three ruffles! And she had a lace ruffle on her neck, and her hair was braided and twisted in a little wad. Well, it was simply dreadful! "I thought I never could stand it till I wrote to you," she concluded.

The teacher began to make inquiry as to Ruth's work. She had no trouble with her, for Ruth had a strong suspicion that she knew a great deal more than the teacher. She sent her to the black-board, and assigned her a task in arithmetic which it seemed that she ought to be able to perform. Ruth looked at it blankly.

"Don't you know how to do that work?"

"No, ma'am."

"What have you done in arithmetic?"

"We have had mostly number work."

"Oh, number work. What did you do in number work?"

"We could add and subtract and multiply

and divide anything without the slate or black-board."

Ruth said this with all the dignity that she could command. It was ridiculous to have those country gawks looking at her as if she didn't know anything when she had always been one of the best in her class. She wished to impress them with the abundance of her knowledge.

"Well, you may sit down and I will see about your arithmetic later."

The fact was that Ruth had been drilled from the primary grade up in the combination of numbers, and her knowledge of arithmetical processes was far behind that of the children in the country school. They called this work the mental discipline of the school, and every teacher firmly believed that this constant drill was increasing the capacity of the pupils for systematic thinking. It stood in striking contrast to the memory work of geography and history. Ruth could add, subtract, multiply and divide with remarkable rapidity.

There are other machines that can do the same.

If one is planning for a life work as a cashier or book-keeper, no doubt the machine method is convenient, but as a means for developing the thinking powers of a child, it is a failure. No child could ever comprehend the component parts of 49. Even a matured mind can not grasp as a whole any quantity beyond 4. As soon as it exceeds this, it must be separated into its parts.

Ruth had learned that six fives make thirty, but that had involved little reasoning power. She had learned the component parts of every number under 100, and of some far beyond it, and she could have gone on indefinitely.

But she had merely learned it:—learned it just as she learned the facts of geography. It was largely memory work after all. Some children can perform this work more quickly than others because they have a readier memory for facts.

PURE FACT—MEMORY IS OFTEN COUNTED FOR MATHEMATICAL ABILITY.

The child that is most apt in number work may lack much of being a good mathematician. Mathematics and numbers are no more related than history and dates.

One is a matter of memory; the other is science.

To understand why one when reduced makes ten of the next lower order requires some degree of logical thought, and the child that has been drilled merely in number work has not had the right discipline for its comprehension.

This number work has always held a higher place in the education of children than it deserves, but at present some of our educators are going frantic over it.

Fortunately for Ruth, the teacher had patience and tact, and though the scornful little nose was in the air at the beginning of the lessons, she was soon working diligently, and for the first time in her life impressed with the idea that she was personally responsible for learning the thing assigned her. She was getting real mental development in those months as she came in contact with a teacher who had the rare faculty of teaching children.

It was a revelation to Ruth that there could be anything of worth in a woman who had an evident scorn for "style" and who forgot her complexion to such an extent that she would stand in the sunshine and play "anti-over" with the children.

It is our misfortune that the law of supply and demand that governs the trade markets does not, and can not, give us enough natural teachers; teachers that like the poets are born and not made. This young woman did not get this faculty for putting herself in sympathy with the various natures of the children under her charge from any institute or Normal School, although she had some knowledge of their methods. The Institutions of Method may multiply themselves in vain in their efforts to mould into true teachers the greater part of the clay that comes into their hands. We must take what we can get to fill the vacant places, but certain it is, there is not enough material to go round.

Ruth found on the play ground, as well as in the school room, a new delight in free, unaffected natures. After the first painfully embarrassing days were past, when Ruth stood in silent disdain of these uncultured children, and they somewhat in awe of her, when she had not a confidant to whom she could ridicule them, and she was compelled to be friends at last, her bright blue eyes and golden curls opened the way for her into each boyish heart.

A bunch of the first violets, or a young robin that had been captured on its first excursion from its nest, or the ripest, reddest strawberries, were brought and shyly offered to her.

Katie was delighted with every attention that was given to her pretty cousin. Her

own nature was steeped in that loveliness
that includes all humanity in its affection.

When she grew to womanhood they
called her "motherly."

But while those little country boys liked
her, not one of them would give his pet
squirrel to see her smile.

By and by Ruth began to forget that there
was so much of a difference in their social
standing. As the out-door sport began to
develop a latent power for enjoyment, she
would for long hours completely forget to
be "stylish," and actually learned to scream
with real girlish delight.

It was in the fall that Auntie May came
into the country to visit her brother's family. She confessed herself shocked to see
Ruth. "Who ever could have believed that
a child could change so? I always thought
her a wonderfully stylish child. She had
such an air. Now she moves along just like
any common child."

Grandma Stebbins did not like this talk

before Ruth. It had a false ring to her honest ears.

"We think the child has improved very much in the country. She is surely health-ier."

Auntie May had little interest in a question of so small importance as a child's health, and she gave little heed to grandma's remark. "Can it be possible that that is Ruth!"

And Auntie May held up her hands as she heard a scream, and saw Ruth mounting high up in the branches of the locust, as her big cousin ran under the swing.

"When she was with me I never knew her to do anything so rude. She was such a lady. I hoped, when I came out here, to get her started in music, but of course she will have to wait now until the folks move. She can't practice on that old organ. I am going to send her my piano. I expect to have a new one."

"Has Ruth any gift for music?" grandma inquired.

"One can't tell how much she may have; but we'll have her practice faithfully for a few years, and we will find out. One don't require much gift if one is diligent."

In accordance with Auntie May's program, one of the first things after the family were settled in the city again was to hunt a music teacher, and Ruth was set to do tread-mill service at the piano.

The morning hours were always too full for practice, and the time that Ruth promised faithfully to allot to the exercise was just after school, from four o'clock to five. From day to day she drummed away at this hour. Evidently no spark of the divine fire had lodged in her soul, but the finger exercises, the scales and amusements were devotedly gone over and over until every member of the household fairly shivered when they heard the first note of the practice hour.

Parson Weaver in his study would scowl, and feel an intense impulse to order the piano shut; but the thought that his daughter, like any other young lady with aspirations, must learn to play on the piano, restrained him.

The neighbors heard that iterated "trum-trum" until they would have felt delight if a bonfire had taken off all the pianos that were ever made.

But no matter; it began at ten years of age and lasted regularly until twenty-two, and intermittently for years after, and to no one concerned was it ever anything but "trum-trum." To no one at least except the music teacher who was putting Auntie May's dollars into her pocket.

In the name of all that is reasonable, why not make the girls mount birds, or train dogs, or write poems, or carve statues, or do some work that requires skill, as well as keep them everlasting pounding on a piano? It would crucify the feelings of those around them less, it would be of just as much value to the girls, it would be less injurious to their health, and would cost far less money.

Blessed be the memory of the woman who

will bring our girls and their foolish parents
to a realizing sense of the folly of forcing
every girl, irrespective of aptitude, to play
the piano. But the piano drumming had
just begun. After a few weeks Ruth became acquainted with the "stylish" girls in
school.

The afternoon hour was soon devoted to
amusement in their company, and the prac-
ticing was crowded into the evening. Tired,
nervous and cross, she played the finger
exercises, the scales and the amusements
over and over again.

Understand, this was done of her own
free will; she needed neither compulsion
nor urging; and all this not because of the
least love of the art, but because it was "the
proper thing."

After a while came recitals, when people
came to hear music. Some came because
their daughters were going to play; some
because they loved music.

And how many of the twenty young girls
who were to entertain them had any trace of

the divine gift? Certain it is that a great
many did not. They played the selections
that they had practiced for many weary
hours, and the audience sat in polite endurance. A sigh of relief and faint applause
followed their efforts.

Their music was not a delight, and they
paid for it with time and strength and
nerve power that might have equipped them
with attainments of real value to them.

The ennobling influence of music can
hardly be over-estimated, but it is good
music that ennobles, and not the mechani-
cally acquired parody on it. As well set
every girl in the country to writing poetry
for one hour each day, and compel the rest
of us to read it, as to have the air filled with
the notes of this universal, indiscriminate
and everlasting piano practice.

There may be some excuse for mistakes
in estimating the capacity of a child for
some things, but the aptitude for music,
or the lack of it, manifests itself in the early
years, and to allow a child to expend months

of time and stores of nervous energy in a futile effort to become a real musician,—what is it if not folly? To force a child to do so,—what is it if not cruelty? But Ruth would have sacrificed a great deal for her piano practice. Not to do the thing that the other girls did, or not to dress as they dressed would be everlasting disgrace.

When the sewing girl came to the parsonage, if the little garments were not fashioned with proper sleeve and collar, there was sure to be a battle.

"I shall be mortified to death to wear that old fashioned thing. I know Auntie May would think it just dreadful for me to go to school looking as if I came from the country."

The sewing girl had once interposed with, "Little girls ought to wear what their mothers think best. I am sure when I was a little girl I would have thought this a very nice dress to wear to school."

"No doubt you would," was Ruth's significant reply, and she drew her mother into the next room to have the discussion alone. Now strange it may seem, but the most potent argument that decided the mother in Ruth's favor was that effort of the seamstress to convince Ruth that the dress was good enough for her. All the mother's impulses rushed to the child's relief. Who can analyze that mother instinct, that upon the least opposition to the child, lets judgment go to the winds, and arrays all her forces on the side of the child?

Ruth understood this, and she knew that her mother would yield in time if there were but tears and grief enough.

And the seamstress knew it, too, and laid aside the disputed piece of goods.

"The idea, mamma! How I shall look! And she seems to think there is no difference between her and me. Do you want me to look as if I were going to be a sewing girl? Auntie May says I have a place to make in society, and that my clothes ought to have some care. And Beatrice has a lovely new henrietta with lined sleeves. It's

just lovely. And I have to wear those little skimpy sleeves. Oh, dear." Another
shower of tears.

"Why, those will be quite nice. I wouldn't
feel so badly about it, dear. If you behave
yourself prettily and are a good girl, no
one will think any the less of you if your
sleeves are not so large." She might just
as well have used this argument with a
girl of sixteen. Ruth knew better than her
mother that that statement was not true
with regard to the girls who were her associates. She would not be held in as high
esteem. The circumference of her sleeve
was a matter of vital importance. Her
mother talked to her as if she were merely
a normally developed child. As if her
thoughts and feelings were those of a child
such as she herself had been at ten years,
or as was the judge's little daughter who
slept with her dollies and rolled a hoop.

She was far from right. It would have
been a crucifixion of her feelings to have
been compelled to wear clothes different

from those of her companions. There were enough girls in the school who still wore gingham aprons, but they were girls whom Ruth felt to be her social inferiors. She felt these things just as keenly as if she had been as matured in body as in mind. There was nothing to her in life to be more desired than to be considered as belonging to the "proud and stylish" set, and it was just as real to her as it was to her admired Auntie May.

The tears and pleading prevailed.

The mother went back to the sewing-room, and trying to hide any consciousness of having been defeated, said:

"You may put that piece in the sleeves. I will get a new piece of velvet for the bertha."

"Very well," was all the seamstress answered; but she told the family at home that evening that the importance of that stuck-up little Ruth was something ridiculous.

She had the feelings and aspirations of a

girl years her senior, and the matter of dress was only one of the ways in which they showed themselves. But this was not the most offensive way. Had her mother seen her on the school ground, even her blinded eyes would have been opened to the fact that there was something vitally wrong in the development of her child. With her own ideas of maidenly propriety, ideas that had been handed down to her from generations of modest women, she would have been shocked at the moral deformity, if she could have realized the real feelings and motives that prompted Ruth and her girl friends in their behavior.

The girls in gingham aprons could be found playing "Old Pompey is dead," or even "Crack the Whip," but the exclusive set were far beyond that. They arranged themselves in couples, and set out to attract the attention of the boys on the opposite side. They first promenaded the sidewalk, arm in arm, and talked and laughed with all imaginable coquettish airs.

Had the boys been as forward in their development as they were, they would have had less trouble, but fortunately the ball game and the marbles held more attraction for them than girls did. Occasionally one would answer the challenge, and come and talk to them, but their judgment had not developed with their desire for admiration and attention, and they were not at all timid about following the boys into the playground, and insisting upon having their attention.

Out of school hours the set had their small parties; not as a company of children, to play "hide and seek" or "pussy wants a corner," and go home at twilight. They went in the evening, each girl waiting at her home until called for by her "regular company." Then at ten or eleven they came home together in the same way. Their games and amusements were highly savored with sentiment and effusiveness. Wherever they happened to be, they collected in little groups, and talked and laughed in painful imitation of eighteen-year-old girls.

After school hours they went arm in arm, inventing errands to bring them into contact with the clerks, who were much more attentive and susceptible than the school boys of their own age; or they stood in the postoffice and simpered their nonsense in high, strident tones, and posed with affected airs; they filled in all the vacant time with excessive giggling, or stood with eyes filled with admiration and envy for every fashionably dressed woman who passed; or they would follow the school boys, insisting upon having attention from them.

Amongst themselves there were the same jealousies that exist amongst older ones. It was deplorable to see little girls with bitter feelings toward a companion when she succeeded in attracting an undue amount of attention; and these occasions were more frequent than with older girls, for the boys who were susceptible to these things were much fewer in number than the girls. When every device for prolonging their stay had been tried, they reluctantly strolled home.

All this performance was an outward expression of an inward condition. Were this the worst of this unnatural life, the results are still to be deplored. But there is too often an under-current in the life of these children that is unknown and unsuspected by all except an occasional observing and thoughtful mother.

WhenRuth's mother first heard, at the W. C. T. U. meeting, that there was a bad condition of morals among the children of the public schools, she was surprised that she had never seen nor heard anything of this. Then came the comforting thought that her children knew nothing about it. The lady who spoke had said "amongst some of the children," and of course Ruth did not associate with such. It must be the Polish children of whom these things were true. "It is so unfortunate" she remarked "that our children are compelled to go to school in a mass."

It had required some courage on the part of the lady who made the statement to introduce the subject.

She continued that she hoped that the Union would see that it was their duty to do something about the matter.

"But we don't know anything definitely about it," the president replied. "There have been floating reports of this kind, but there seem to be no certain facts."

"I do know of certain facts that make the matter clear enough to me."

"In that case, why do you not go to the principal and tell him?"

"Well, ladies, now that the question has been asked, I will tell you the whole story. I did go to the principal not long ago. It was not a pleasant task, I assure you. I told him what I believed, and some of the things that had led me to think it. He let me tell the whole thing without a word, but I could plainly see by the expression on his face his opinion of a woman who could ever have such thoughts about children, or who could relate them to a man. After I had said all that I considered it my duty to say, he waited a full minute so as to properly impress me, and then said: 'Well, madam, as you are so convinced of the truth of what you say, I suppose that you are prepared to prove the truth of all these assertions.'

"I had gone to him with my information because of an overpowering sense of duty. I answered him:

"'I am not prepared to do anything of the kind. If after I have told you these things you can not go to work and find out the truth of them, I shall feel at least that I have done my duty.'

"'Do not trouble yourself on that score, madam,' he answered. 'As far as you are responsible for my school, you have certainly done your whole duty.'

"My husband said, when I came home and told him about it, that it served me right; that I might have minded my own business.

"I have said nothing about it since, but I

live just back of the school house, and I see
so much that I felt compelled to say something."

"Well, what can we do? If the teacher
will not listen, shall we go to the board?"

"Yes, if you are prepared to prove everything that you are morally convinced of."

"Well, shall we go to the parents?"

"Go to the parents! Well, I guess not, if
you don't expect to be eternally ostracized
from their society."

Then Ruth's mother spoke.

"Well, you would not care for that. They
are a class of society that our Union ought
to be interested in, and do the best for,
whether they appreciate it or not."

There was a smile on some of the faces at
this speech, and they all realized how difficult it would be to say anything to parents
on the subject.

Without coming to any conclusion, but
wishing, as they had wished many times,
that there might be some women on the
school board who might be approached on

7

such subjects, and who would feel that they
were matters of enough importance to in-
vestigate, they separated. The fact was that
while Ruth belonged to the set of which
these accusations were true, she herself was
not one of the culprits. The intense pride,
that had influenced her in joining the set,
likewise kept her aloof from its coarser
aspects. She came in contact with them, she
knew about them, and her moral sense was
dwarfed, perhaps for all life; but she came
from a clean, Puritan stock, and generations of pure women had given her a heritage that even in these social conditions was
a safeguard.

Ruth had some difficulty in getting all
the time for promenading the streets that
she wanted without exciting her mother's
suspicion. If the hour was very late when
she came from school, she pleaded head-
ache and the need of fresh air.

She was always so lady-like that her
mother never questioned her behavior when
away from her. Besides, she had good

standing in school, her marks were excellent, and to her mother she appeared the very ideal of a girl.

If the girl who is morally in dangerous places would only make such tremendous breaks from the required social standards as the boy will, her danger could be so much more easily discovered and dealt with.

Quite to the contrary, however, she is all the time deporting herself in the most approved and lady-like manner.

In the school Ruth was faithfully doing the required work, for her love of admiration would never permit her to fall behind her classmates.

Oh, this love of admiration, how strong it is in womankind! No woman can be womanly without it. When it is narrowed entirely to personal appearances, and is obnoxiously apparent, we call it vanity; but in its normal condition it is what has made woman lovable under the most trying circumstances. She must be loved whatever else happens, and to be loved is to be admired.

This element was intense in Ruth. If it could have been rightly directed, it would have been the means of developing her into a strong, useful woman; but turned in the wrong direction it would have just the opposite effect.

To appear stupid would not have been so stinging to Ruth, it is true, as to appear common, or what she called vulgar; but she would have made a much greater effort than school requirements demanded to keep a respectable standing in school.

She was in no sense dull. She had an ordinary supply of good brain power, and an unusual amount of pride and ambition. It was her misfortune that she had not had a strong, firm hand to guide her, and she was swept along in the current of public school life that appealed most strongly to her inclinations.

Her mother's hands and heart were crowded with duties. Not that she felt that

her children were neglected. To her a
mother's duty was to care for the bodily
wants of her children, to teach them general and formal Christian duties, and to
send them to school.

She did these things as well as she could.
The little steps were carefully guided. But
it is the little steps that need the least care.
As the children grew older she had no power
to penetrate their secret thoughts, much less
to guide them. She had no power to know
whether the inner spiritual life of the child
was developing roundly and wholesomely.
That word spiritual presents to so many
minds just what it did to Ruth's mother. It
was that element in the human soul that
lit up sister Brown's face when she prayed,
and it would come to her children when
they were old enough if they attended
prayer meeting and other means of its culti-
vation. In the meantime, the real spiritual
life of her daughter was a sealed book to
her.

There was not a genuine bond of sym-

pathy between them. She had never really
invited the confidence of her child. It can
never be forced from any child, and only
comes spontaneously when she feels that influence impelling her to reveal her feelings
that a really congenial soul exerts.

Others may wash and cook and sew for
her, and it is a matter of little importance;
but when another than the mother must be
the girl's best friend, it is a grave misfortune.

"Best friend" does not mean to the girl
just what even Ruth might have thought.
The chattering girl companion did not know
her deepest life. There are deeps and deeps
in the life of a young girl.

Only an older person could ever have
drawn confidences from her that were deepest and most real, and that person had never
yet come into her life.

She had long, long thoughts that were
left all unsettled because she had never
come in contact with any one that called
from her her real, inner life.

Strange, that the mother had so far forgotten the days of her own girlhood, when
the wonderful problems of life were just beginning to present themselves to her. She
had never considered this contact with her
child's life necessary. She had good, time-
honored ideas about her duty. She was
first to be a good housekeeper. Her own
mother had impressed this idea upon her
mind by many a precept and illustration.

She had told her the story of the man
who started out to find a wife. He went
from house to house, asking for crumbs of
dried bread dough from the last week's
bread pan. When finally he was told by
one house-wife that such things never ex-
isted in that house, he said: "It is the
daughter of this house that I want for my
wife."

Also in a book that her father had given
her as a Christmas present she found an
essay or two on "How to Choose a Wife."
The point that was made most vivid to her
girlish mind was the advice to young men

that if, in walking behind a girl, they should see a raveling on her dress, to be sure of one thing, that she was not fitted to be a wife.

Now, no such things as ravelings or dried bread crumbs ever remained unmolested in her house, and she considered herself possessed of one of the great qualifications of motherhood. Housekeeping and motherhood are no more related than gardening and fatherhood.

The most ideal housekeeper may be a complete failure as a mother, and the mother who can keep her daughter's life as close to her as the apple is to the tree, may be very far from perfection in the matter of drawers and closets.

Ruth had gone to her father occasionally when her mother had failed her.

Her preacher father would have been shocked if he could have been aware of the tumult of thoughts that were stirred up in her mind when a visitor replied to a remark of his:

"That is a memory of some former existence. You have lived before, you know."

Her father merely laughed, and Ruth looked at him in doubt, wondering if he really believed that. She was unable to decide, and after much wondering said:

"Papa, were we just made as we are, or have we really lived before, as Mr. Jennings said?"

"Those are no thoughts for a child like you, Ruth. You are not old enough to talk about such things. Leave them alone until you are older."

Why did not the good man add, "and we will explain them to you then?"

In this childish brain, forever busy, there was a turmoil of thoughts that were suggested by the fragments of the conversation of older people.

She was shut out from all real communion by parents who were so convinced that it was their duty to appear wise to their children that they repelled any confidence that was dangerous to this ideal.

The questioning child has always been called the thinking child, but the child that rarely questions is quite as often the thoughtful one.

Ruth was with her mother very little of the time. The school hours were lengthened far into the afternoon, and only rarely did the mother expect any help from her.

Almost apologetically she would say:

"I did need you so much, Ruth, to help take care of the baby. He is so fretful now that he is teething that I haven't been able to do anything since dinner but take care of him. I want you to roll him in his carriage and give him a little fresh air."

"Why can't Mary do that? I don't want to go rolling a baby like a nurse girl."

"Mary has all that she can do in the kitchen. If you had come home in time you might have ironed some of the plain clothes and given her time to take him out."

"Well, I'm just not going to spread my hands doing hired girl's work. I'll take the baby out to the hammock. There is just as much fresh air there as any place."

So unwillingly she took the little fellow out of his mother's aching arms and carried him out to the hammock. He knew the unsympathetic touch, and kicked and screamed in resistance.

"He won't be good with me. I don't know how to take care of babies."

"You might learn with a little more patience, dear."

"I never can learn. I don't want to learn. I wish I lived with Auntie May where they don't have a lot of hateful babies to take care of."

"O, Ruth, don't talk so. Just think what a gift from God our dear baby is."

But Ruth was still unconvinced. She carried the baby with an expression that showed an utter lack of an appreciation of the appropriateness of the gift. Once in the hammock, the little one was jerked back and forth, while Ruth stood wondering why so many of the girls could always have such nice clothes, while she was compelled to battle over each new garment, and do such disagreeable things as to rock babies.

The baby responded to Ruth's mood, and sent forth such wails that it brought the mother to the scene of action.

"Why don't you sit in the hammock with him and be more kind?" the mother suggested patiently.

"I don't see what more I can do. I can swing him better this way."

But the little arms went up and the under lip trembled at the mother's approach in such a pathetic way that Ruth gained her point, and the mother's tired arms once more held the heavy little body.

It was these little victories that were gradually deciding the relation between mother and child. Ruth each day had less respect for her mother's opinion on any subject, and less confidence in her ability to enforce obedience in what she resolutely determined not to do.

Open rebellion would have called for

severe measures; but a weak loving mother was gradually being conquered by a self-willed, selfish child.

In the household, where her hands and feet could have saved her mother so many weary moments, very little was ever demanded of her. Occasionally the father interfered, and insisted on some trifling household duty being performed; but even he relented from his severity when he saw the violet eyes fill with tears, and the pretty lip tremble.

She felt herself abused, and her sweet, feminine beauty appealed even to him, until he gave his tacit consent to a systematic course of training in pure selfishness.

The little hands were kept white, the tapering nails were never broken, and the consideration of herself before all others was regarded as a natural right. Even thus favored, she considered herself abused that she was compelled to do with much less of the world's goods than many of her young friends.

In after years, when the need of her parents' counsels was much more important, when she was too old for punishment or discipline, the parents wondered why, with all their kindness, their child should have such disregard for their wishes.

The thought that Ruth could not always stay under their protecting roof, that she must some day come in contact with a world that would not use her as if she were a petted plaything, did not often occur to these inconsiderate parents. The mother had a dim notion that Ruth's beauty would raise her above the common lot of women. She failed to realize that her daughter's life must, in its phases of responsibility, be in some sense a repetition of her own; that her duties would be a woman's duties, calling for patience, self-sacrificing, and suffering.

It is no doubt a beautiful and poetic idea that these sweet young girls are fair flowers, with no more serious mission than to shed their fragrance and beauty for the delight of mankind. Beautiful it would be, if it were only true. Beauty, however valued and sought, never makes life's duties any lighter for a woman, and there comes a time when she awakens to the fact that she was not created merely to beautify the earth, but to confront its hard and serious duties like the rest of human kind.

It is always a shock, and often a serious one, and she revolts against her destiny only to make herself a burden to society. Of all the teachers into whose hands Ruth came, only one ever realized that these girls needed any special thought or care. They never ran away from school, or told lies, or refused to obey. They never in any way flagrantly disregarded the rules of the school. They were never rude or coarse. In fine, they were the show pupils. Was there an entertainment either in the school or in the Sunday school, these were the ones who were always put forward to speak, to sing, to pose. They were usually the favorites, or as the other girls called them, the "pets," and they accepted the relation as their natural right. The teachers stood somewhat in awe of their criticism.

One woman there was who had been between the mill-stones of life until she had learned their cruel grind to its full extent, who recognized the falseness of their ideals and motives. This woman, who had been left to perform the duties of motherhood to her little ones, and at the same time to earn their daily bread, one day led her little two-year-old into the school room. Many of the girls crowded around her, and tried all their pretty arts of coaxing to attract the little child.

But none of the "swell" set were among them. A patronizing "How cute!" as they passed along was all the attention they deigned to bestow.

"Why does a little child not have the same natural attraction for these girls as for the others?" was her query.

She began to study into their lives. Secretiveness was so much a characteristic with them that this was not an easy matter; but with patience she found that the conversation common among them was of a nature calculated to shock propriety.

Not grossly obscene, it was saturated with suggestiveness.

The woman who could best stifle the maternal instincts was looked upon with admiration as an ideal of "smartness."

They had their young lovers, and billet-doux of the most extravagant nature passed between them.

With infinite tact this teacher began to ingratiate herself into the confidence of these girls. Her babies and the memory of a husband she loved were the sweetest things in life to her, and it appalled her to find that these girls, not yet in their maidenhood, should hold all that these signified in contempt.

Ruth impressed her as being the most susceptible, and she tried with all her art to draw her out with reference to her aims and ideals.

Unfortunately, just as it appeared that she was having some influence, and eliciting some germs of confidence, a new appointment moved the Weaver family to another locality. In a few weeks all impression made by this woman upon Ruth had been effaced. If the nomadic life of her father had not compelled her to leave this woman at this critical period, she might have proved the open sesame to the truer and better nature of the girl.

In another town and another school Ruth found the same set of companions. Wherever she went she never failed to find them. Sometimes they were more numerous, sometimes they were more saturated with these precocious and disastrous sentiments, but she never failed to find them.

The teacher who had discovered what was the life and the ideal of these girls brought the matter up a little later at a teachers' meeting in as direct a way as she dared. The principal looked at her a moment as if she had completely lost her senses, and then changed the subject to the consideration of the best method to regulate the match games of base ball.

She did not allude to it again, yet she felt that it was a theme that needed serious thought.

When Ruth again entered school she had left her girlhood behind her, and was standing on the threshold of her maidenhood.

MAIDENHOOD.

"Standing with reluctant feet,
Where the brook and river meet."

Ruth did not stand with reluctant feet; she was eager to go on. The years before her contained no mystery. The period that is the heritage of the natural girl, the beautiful wonder-age that poetry has called "sweet sixteen," would never become a part of her life. She would have to go back to her childhood to find the shy timidity that usually comes to girls when they find themselves for the first time the objects of admiration and attention. The sudden realization of this that sends the hand involuntarily to the hair to tuck a curl into place, or give the long braids a swing, or press a rebellious hair pin into the ambitious coiffure; the apprehensive glance at the toe of the shoe, the sudden straightening of the waist and pressing down of the belt, and

the faint blush of pink that betrays the fact
that the girl realizes her young womanhood,
these were the things that would not come
to Ruth.

She stopped before each mirror that happened in her way, but not with that quick,
stolen glance that betrays such consciousness.

It was done deliberately, and she turned
away with the satisfied toss of the head that
shows experience and gratified pride. She
spent a long time before her own little glass
before she considered her toilet complete
the first morning that she started for school.

"Why do you take so long to dress yourself, Ruth? You would look just as well if
you spent less time, and I did hope that you
could help me a little this morning."

"You know the first morning counts for
so much, mamma. I'm sure I can't go to
school and work too. Auntie May always
told me to make a good first impression, for
it was worth everything."

It was a very fair, slender girl that presented herself at the door of the high school that September morning. She had not the straight shapeless form so commonly seen in girls, for corsets and infinite care with puff and ruffle and pleat had aided much in giving her a womanly appearance.

She looked the principal over with a cool criticism that made him feel a trifle uncomfortable.

What was there in that first moment of meeting that made the principal mentally decide that the new preacher's daughter would not be a desirable accession to his school, and caused Ruth to draw herself to her highest when she met his glance, and write to her girl friends that she knew he would be "just horrid?"

There was a sort of instinctive antagonism between the two, and each recognized in the other a power that was to be dreaded.

When Ruth told at home that she did not like her new teacher, she found it very difficult to tell why.

"O, he laughs horrid; and he keeps one foot going whenever he sits down."

She had not analyzed the case sufficiently to realize that the absence of any admiring glance was what she missed.

Never before, from the time that she had cried for her brown slippers to the present, had she come under a teacher whom she could not influence with a sweet smile and a bright coquettish air.

But this teacher was a masculine "old maid" in his very nature. He tolerated the girls in his school because the law allowed them there, but he was always surprised if they made a creditable recitation.

And they never did their best. He was constantly insinuating their inferiority; at the end of every question asked of a girl there was an inflection indicating that it would probably not be answered. The girls in his school always caused him more trouble than the boys. Even Ruth, in whom the spirit of mischief did not predominate, took delight in annoying him.

When at their first meeting she realized how little impression her girlish charms had on him, she immediately concluded that at some former time he had been disappointed in a love affair. She could imagine no other cause for his callousness.

He had been in the school for many years, and had taught the parents of the boys and girls now under his charge, but he had never discovered that the way to govern the girl is through her pride and her affection. In fact he gave her little thought. He would have abolished her if he could, and being unable to do that he endured with a very poor grace her presence in his school, and she always with his co-operation degenerated from any former standing as a scholar.

In the early history of the town there had been all preparation for a "boom," and it was a matter of some speculative importance when the school board met to decide upon the location of the new school building that was to supersede the earlier temporary one.

"We want it where it will show up well,"
one of the "city fathers" remarked.

"Yes, certainly, if we put all this money
into a school we must have something that
will show up big in the advertising pamphlets. There is nothing in the world that
will advertise a town and bring in people
like a fine school building. We want it
where it will show up well."

"I tell you, the bluffs is just the place."

"Too far out, isn't it?"

"Not a bit. Just what the little fellows
need. Won't hurt them a bit more than to
play ball all that time."

"Take a little of the mischief out of them,
hey?" with an appeal to the principal who
had been called in for consultation.

"O, that's all right," and that worthy gave
a knowing laugh calculated to impress the
board with the fact that he could attend to
such small matters without any aid.

The discussion went on. Plans were
laid before them by the special committee,
and the size and cost of arch, column and

cupola received due consideration. What they could afford in fancy stone for trimming, and finally the heating apparatus were discussed.

There was some suggestion that stoves would be more economical, but this suggestion was laughed to scorn. How could stoves be advertised in the pamphlet? As an afterthought, and in the face of the opposition of the stove advocate, who thought it would be a waste of heat, a system of ventilation was decided upon.

It was a long time before the subject of location was finally settled. The man who owned property on the heights and the man who favored an extension of the town in that direction were very firmly convinced that the bluffs afforded the most advantageous situation in all respects, and all agreed that for "showing up" purposes it could have no equal.

There was one faint, lone objection.

"The children can't climb that hill in winter."

"O, that's nothing. We can put in some steps in the worst places with very little expense."

To be sure. That was just the thing. Steps would fix things all right. And the property owner and the extension man would be glad, and how that building would "show up" from Main Street, and Dinwiddie Street, and the Park, and the depot!

Yes, the bluffs was the place.

"School house location is fixed," said one member of the board to his wife, as he returned home.

"Where is the location?"

"Up on the bluffs."

"On the bluffs? Are you men crazy?"

"Crazy? No madam. We are not crazy. Magnificent show from Main Street and the Depot. Just the thing for our advertising pamphlet."

"Why, papa, what are you thinking of? You know Mabel cannot climb that hill, and she will be in the high school next year."

"Well, I couldn't bring personal consid-
erations into the discussion of an important
subject like that."

Dear man, of course he couldn't for he
never thought of it. He had very carefully
considered expenses, extensions, town
"boom," advertising pamphlets, and (inci-
dentally and collectively) even "the little
fellows;" but his own delicate daughter, and
what it might mean to her had never occurred to him nor to any other man on that
board.

To the mother it came as the first and
controlling consideration, but what of that?

The school house went up on the bluffs;
and it presented a beautiful appearance
from Main Street, and Dinwiddie Street,
and the Park, and the depot, and in the
pamphlet.

There were twice as many girls as boys
in the high school, yet their peculiar needs
had never been the object of consideration
for a moment. In fact it had never occurred to those men that girls of that age

have peculiar needs. Had they been pillars, or fancy trimming stone, or even a stair railing, they would have come in for a share of consideration.

But what did it mean to those girls, who for the first four years of their womanhood, were compelled to climb that hill and the two flights of stairs that had to be mounted before the high school room was reached?

It meant increased back-ache and head-ache, weak eyes, over-taxed nerves, palpitating heart, disordered stomach, and every other evil that follows in the train of that insidious disease that has settled down on the American women.

The hill and the long stairs were not alone responsible for it; it exists in every public school in America; but these things impose conditions on the girls that augment their troubles, and make them wrecks of womanhood when they pose as "sweet girl graduates."

The daughters of the land have a right to expect on the part of the individuals who have charge of their education some knowledge of their needs; but it is a deplorable fact that the ordinary member of the school board cares little, and knows less, about the subject.

He pays the doctor bills of his wife and daughter with the readiness of the indulgent American husband and father. He expects to do it. That is one of the unfortunate features of the subject. Our women and girls are sick so much that the men expect it as a part of the price they pay for the privilege of having a wife.

That there is a cause for it for which they are partly responsible would be an amazing revelation to them. If the men will insist upon the exclusive control of the school boards, it would be no more than fair that they have some proper knowledge of the need of the majority of the pupils of our high schools.

The fact that the proportion of our women who are sick is nine in every ten would be a surprise to them; but it is a fact, and it is a matter of grave importance to understand the cause.

In Europe the statement has been made that the climate of our country is unhealthy because our women are in such a diseased condition. Why, the Indian women lived here for centuries, went through all the vicissitudes of maternity, and there was no army of doctors or swarm of patent medicine men deriving their sustenance from them. Our men dismiss the subject with "O, it is the way you live!" No doubt it is; but how do we live? What is it in our lives that makes them radically different from the lives of our grandmothers? Why is it that a foreign woman, not from the class who work in the field, but from the good middle class, will bring up a family of girls in this country, living in the home just about such a life as she did in Europe, maintaining her own health unimpaired through years of American conditions, and yet find these daughters the same physical wrecks when they come to years of womanhood, as the American woman is? One vital point of difference is the public school. The public schools of America are largely responsible for the ruined constitutions of American women.

What! Shall woman, just as she has demonstrated the long-disputed fact that she is capable of the same education as a man, confess that in order to do it she must wreck her health and happiness?

No, she need not confess that; but she must confess that the system of education onto which she has been grafted is unsuited to her needs.

That there must be a great deal of knowledge and many new ideas acquired by our school boards; that there must be many new elements introduced into our school system; that the needs of the girls, as well as the needs of the boys, must have study; and that women teachers must assert themselves to get thought and attention from the men, must be recognized before she can properly acquire her education.

This school in which Ruth started in her critical age was one of the worst of its kind, but unfortunately it is multiplied many times in every state. What she really needed was a system of education that should be physical as well as mental. It was absolutely necessary to her proper development. She needed it more than any boy in school. Why did she not have it? Was not the play ground as free to her as to the boy? Certainly it was; but custom with its crushing hand has ruled out of the life of every girl, who has passed beyond the child period, any part in any game that will in the least call for physical exertion. It would seem as if every effort were being made on the part of those in charge of our girls to make the conditions of her education as unfavorable as possible.

There were days when the nervous strain should have been lightened; when warmth and quiet were the first essentials to her well-being; but what did her teacher know of these things?

Ruth had started into school with all her old ambition to be first. To her great surprise she found herself responsible for learning the lessons that were assigned her. She had been taught for so many years, that the habit of learning was very difficult for her. It called for unusual exertion at the age when she had little vitality to expend, but there was little chance of lightening the stress when it bore too heavily, for there was no elasticity in the system.

One wet morning when Ruth started on her long tramp up the hill, her mother protested.

"You ought not to go to school to-day, Ruth. It really is not right. I wish you would lie down on the couch and keep warm and quiet."

"Why, mamma Weaver! How can I? Don't you know I will get an absent mark, and that will bring down my grade? I should certainly fall into the second division, and then the grade of our room wouldn't stand first if any of us stay out."

"But you are not able to do it. At any rate I will write a note to the teacher, and see if you can not sit where it is warm."

"Why, the idea! I wouldn't do such a thing for the world. I can get along just as well as the other girls."

And half sick and irritable she started for school. She climbed the long slippery hill, and dragged herself wearily up the stairs. Her skirts were wet, and remained so through the morning. When school called, she felt exhausted and nervous; her lessons were failures, and she was unusually trying to the gentleman in charge. The girls were always more difficult for him to manage than the boys; he could not use his hickory ferule on them for one thing; and when Ruth had twisted and turned, and whispered beyond what he was accustomed to endure, he said:

"Take the platform, Miss Weaver."

She hesitated a moment, then bit her lip and walked to the platform. The teacher went on with his work. He was explaining a long problem in algebra, and had completely forgotten the girl on the platform, when the whole school was startled by the sound of a fall, and he turned to see Ruth lying face down on the platform. He went to her, and with the help of one of the boys lifted her into the cloak room and sent for a carriage to take her home. He was exceedingly annoyed. That was not the first time such a thing had happened. He saw no sense in it. The girl had deserved punishment; she had acted abominably.

What that had meant to every girl that he had sent to the platform in his long career, the suffering he had caused, he never imagined. His ferule would have been far preferable. No man who is unmarried, or has not had a course in medicine, has any right to have charge of girls of that age.

The next day Ruth was at school again, a trifle pale, but otherwise appearing as usual. It had been a hard fight, but the grade had been saved. The fear of losing rank, of falling below first place in respect to attendance had been so systematically drilled into these girls, that such inconsiderable things as head-ache and back-ache could not keep them at home.

The Epworth League were to have a "Gipsy Social" that night, and Ruth was to be the queen. When evening came she dressed herself in the required costume, with arms and neck bare, and feet just caught in white slippers, and went out to the lawn where the crowd was gathered.

"Why, my dear child! What are you thinking of? You will catch your death of cold. Do wear your shoes and something over your shoulders if you must go out in that wet grass!" her mother said.

"How I would look! A Gipsy Queen with a shawl on! I should disgrace the whole affair."

"Well, that would be better than to be sick."

"I shan't be sick. There is no use in you fussing so."

And Ruth continued her preparations without paying the least attention to her mother's advice. She was now too old to be compelled to do what was unpleasant to her, and the time was long past when she could have been convinced that her mother's judgment was superior to her own.

Ruth played the queen to perfection, and was the most charming of all the tinsel-bedecked maidens. So much did she enjoy the compliments and attention that she received, that she forgot that there was such a thing as weariness.

It was there, as it is everywhere, the plain girls were dishing the ice cream or doing some useful, inconspicuous work, while Ruth and her set, under the beautiful canopy, were the center of attraction.

It was not until the crowd began to go home and the work of clearing up was at hand, that Ruth began to realize how miserable she felt.

"Girls, I certainly can't stay any longer to help with that work. I'm almost dead."

The girls were not at all surprised at this. It was much like Ruth's usual way; and after some few remarks that were too near the truth to be uttered in Ruth's presence, they went on with their work. When she was in her own room, and all necessity for exertion was over, she realized that her feet were wet, and that the slight chill she had felt for the last hour had given way to a burning fever. In the morning Ruth found that she had more than weariness to contend with, and the doctor was called. He gave an opiate and remarked indifferently that those troubles were quite common with girls. So mother and daughter accepted it as part of the price of womanhood. That many things had led up to it, and that it all might have been prevented, did not seem to be considered.

But for all her life Ruth Weaver, like thousands of her sisters, was paying the penalty of the utter absence of thought on the part of those who had her life in charge.

She was ignorant; her mother was faint-

ly persuaded that it might have been prevented; the doctor was politic and discreet;
and the teacher was indifferent.

The whole muscular system had been allowed to degenerate, because it had no
proper exercise. While the boys were on
the play ground, she was sitting on the
stair-way or in the school room or walking
up and down the side-walk.

In the winter the boys went into the vacant story above, where a gymnasium had
been arranged for them. By special per-
mission the girls were occasionally allowed
to visit it and watch the boys show off their
acrobatic acts, but not one of them even
expressed a desire to perform any of those
feats. Only the wildest ever dared entertain
the secret thought.

Why did not the authorities who provided a gymnasium for the boys, have like consideration for the girls? Every girl there
who was to fulfill the mission of maternity
would need all the strength of muscle and
nerve she could possibly get. But she did

not get it, and what is worse, she did not want it. The healthful play spirit was largely crushed out of her, and her muscles were so flaccid that action held no delight for her. When the time came that this muscular strength was absolutely needed she was physically undone, and had passed into the ever increasing ranks of sick American mothers.

The girl ought to find some muscular developing power in the performance of the household duties. Nothing of this nature was ever expected of Ruth. She was not different in this respect from many of the other girls of the school. Her time was crowded so full of many other duties that very little was left for the performance of household tasks even had she felt thus inclined. She had become habituated to being waited upon. The mother patiently performed the servant's part, and indulgent to the caprices of the daughter, she encouraged her in the various engagements that were more congenial to her taste.

On Monday night the literary society of the high school met, and Ruth was one of the most enthusiastic members. Tuesday evening was appointed for the chorus class. After the hour of practice her "set" went off in couples to spend the rest of the evening together. On Wednesday evening there was choir practice and Sunday school teachers' meeting, and she was connected with both choir and Sunday school.

A girl of sixteen is really just about ready to enter upon a comprehensive study of the Bible, and if she is assigned her most appropriate place she will be found in a class under the direction of a person of mature judgment. On the contrary Ruth and five or six of her mates had charge of classes of children that were getting their first impressions of Bible truths in the most distorted manner from these immature, undisciplined teachers.

The ideas of heaven with its pearly gates and throne of gold were impressed in such a graphic style that to her last day the little girl's imagination always pictured it in the same way, regardless of anything that reason might wish to substitute.

The stereotyped strangeness and stiffness and monotony of it was rather effective in dampening their childish ardor for occupancy, and all the fierceness of the terrors of the only alternative had to be graphically pictured before it could be made reasonably alluring. But these young teachers were usually equal to that too. When they felt moved to inquire into the spiritual condition of their little charges they would ask impressively:

"Mary, don't you want to go to heaven?"

When the old picture rose before Mary's mind, and she showed no active eagerness for immediate translation, the question was changed to:

"Well, surely you don't want to go to hell, do you?" in most awful tones.

The result was a very decided preference on Mary's part for the right here and now as about the best thing going.

But the young teacher was complacent. She had done her duty.

On Thursday evening, at her father's urgent desire, she was usually at prayer meeting. Friday night was supposed to be free, but in reality it was the most crowded night in the week. It was on this night that the "set" had their parties or sleigh rides or moonlight picnics; and on Friday night the church socials of numerous kinds called for work and attendance; or the class in piano music had their term recital. So, very little time was left for mother and daughter to spend together, had they been accustomed to find in each other's society the pleasure and profit that each ought to have received from the other; but they lived so much in this outside world, that the real home life did not exist at all. Ruth's home was the place where she staid over night, or came to practice and to eat.

Although Ruth was at home very little of the time, she usually retired under pretense of lessons either to her room or to some quiet spot. But not all this time was spent in study. One of her constant companions was a story book. Every stray quarter hour was appropriated, and when the book became intensely interesting, the lamp was set on a chair beside her bed, and she read until her eyes stung, and the letters swam before them.

These were not books that she had drawn from the Sunday school library. They were not spiced and seasoned enough for her taste. "An Old-Fashioned Girl," or "We Girls," or any other book that portrayed the life of the normal, well-balanced girl were tame affairs for which she found neither time nor inclination. In short, they were too healthy. She wanted something with a hectic flush. The books that were so eagerly devoured by lamp light, and found a resting place under her pillow told of girls who were girls in years but women in experience; who were once poor, but either in the course of the story or at its close came into the possession of lavish fortunes.

They were always "radiantly beautiful." Who was ever genius enough or reckless enough to create a heroine out of an absolutely plain woman?

They were always passionately loved, often by a stoic of a man who had heretofore been proof against all of Cupid's wiles; or, still more likely by a deep dyed villain who had been miraculously reformed the very first time he had gazed upon her refulgent beauty. And then forever after he devoted himself to her happiness and lavished his wealth upon her; for of course he had wealth.

The absurdity of it all never dawned upon the girl. She eagerly drank in volume after volume. It was rarely that a week went by in which she did not finish one of these books. She lived with the characters in her day dreams as she mounted the long hill to the school, and talked with her school friends about their fortunes as the books went round among them.

There were several shelves of these books

in the public library with worn covers and pages covered with thumb marks and now and then a tear stain. On the afternoons that the library was open the girls met there and exchanged books and opinions.

"O, this is perfectly lovely!" or "This is simply elegant!"

"O, take this one. It's perfectly grand!"

All superlatives were scarcely enough to express their appreciation.

But loss of time and eye-sight was the least harm that resulted from this style of reading.

From these books she got her ideal of life. The every-day life about her was tame and common-place, and not at all what it ought to be in the way of high colors.

The humble parsonage home; her young brothers and sisters; the plain clothes; the friends the family knew; were not all these surroundings and associates ill suited to a girl of her high colored ideals? Was she not unjustly chained down to a prosy hum-drum colorless life with which she could

have no sympathy? The more she compared them with the people and things in
the books, the more she despised them.

The thought of the lovers with the dear,
dark eyes and lofty carriage and the magnificent homes made her at times carry herself
with a cold and haughty bearing toward the
high school boy who was so bashfully trying to pay his attentions to her.

It was only when she was out from under
the spell of the story that she could coolly
reason that his father was probably the richest man in the county, and that to snub the
devoted son was not the part of worldly
wisdom.

But all idea of real manly and maidenly
love, of the appreciation of what is true and
noble was regularly choked out of this artificial life.

The dime novel, the synonym of pernicious literature for the boy, has received so
much attention that the fact that girls have
a style of literature that exactly corresponds
to it seems to have escaped notice.

They are both injurious because they present false pictures of life. They fire the young reader with the ambition to be great in just the same way that the hero or heroine is great. The boy's hero is great in feats of strength and daring. The girl's heroine is great in the fact of grace and beauty. With the boy this comes at an age when the performance of a few foolhardy feats, even disgraceful ones, will represent its full expression.

With the girl it comes at a time when it may lead her to commit acts that will color her whole life.

A lover with a moral character just a little doubtful is so much more romantic than the common, every-day, good young man whom the parents approve; and even if, as in the case of Ruth, the desire to be aristocratic would prevent from anything savoring of disgrace, yet her ideals were modeled upon the pictures of life that she found there.

Her mother need not be equipped "with

a little hoard of maxims preaching down a daughter's heart."

For years she had had it fully arranged in her own mind that she would marry only a rich man. There might be other desirable qualifications, but wealth was absolutely necessary to the winning of her affections. She took it for granted that the beauty and noble bearing of the hero of the books were somehow or other in the kindness of unseen fortune going to be added unto these.

She understood the full nature and value of her own beauty, and knew all the little arts of the coquette before she was out of her teens.

She often tried them on the high school boys with such startling success that she longed for the time to come when the restraints of the preacher's home would be done away with, and she would be free to move in the society that her imagination painted and her soul longed for. She could find no one among her companions worthy

of her steel, and with more and more eagerness she looked forward to the time of her
graduation and her year with Auntie May.
Many a hard lesson she learned with the
sole thought in the learning of it that some
day she would move in brilliant society, and
in brilliant society one must not be ignorant.

Her father would sometimes say:

"You will have to earn your own living,
Ruth. I can keep you in school until you
graduate; then you will have to do something for yourself."

Ruth would answer with dignity:

"I suppose I can."

But she mentally resolved that the time
would be short.

While she lived in this artificial world of
her imagination, she was densely ignorant
of the real world around her. Her mother
had never spoken one word to her that
could not be repeated in the presence of the
whole family. It was her ideal of modesty
never to speak on any subject that required

privacy. The relations between mother and daughter in this respect were so strained, that Ruth would have gone to almost any one for information sooner than to her mother.

The mother had once been as ignorant as Ruth of many of the motives in human nature. She was wiser now, yet she allowed her daughter to remain as she was to get her knowledge as best she might from contact with humanity.

Could she have read with Ruth one of those books that captivated her fancy, she might have shown her that the hero who had led the reckless life was a polluted man, whom ages of reformation would not render a fit mate for the young and beautiful bride that he always won. There was a world of knowledge that her mother could have opened up to her in regard to any one of these books. She called this feeling of reluctance to talk freely with her own child modesty. It was not modesty at all.

It was a distorted idea of God's plans in regard to creation.

Girls demand, and will have in some form, this story of conquest by love. If they can have it where it is true to life and free from the pestilential atmosphere of passion and vice, it is a wonderful power in moulding their ideals and their lives.

Their desire for books is almost insatiate, and the mother who searches through literature for the proper reading for her daughter becomes soon aware that it is one of the fields of literature that is not crowded. To make a story that is strong without being passionate; rich without being untrue; representing virtue and vice in their proper relations without obtruding a moral, requires a gift that is rare. The girl of a fervid nature despises what appears to her childish, and is injured by a promiscuous reading of literature designed for a discriminating age.

Give her free, undirected access to a public library, and like a needle to the pole she will gravitate to that corner where the worn covers and soiled backs announce their character before they are ever opened.

There may be a morbid element in this tendency, but it is so common to girls, and to our brightest and most attractive girls, that it must be seriously admitted that there is some natural common cause for it.

It is confined, in the properly developed girl, to a short period. But during this time, when certain elements in her nature are most active, she craves this kind of sensational literature, and usually finds it.

The time that Ruth appropriated for this reading was not taken by any means at the sacrifice of her school work. She still maintained her standing in the school, but in order to do this as well, she was obliged to do hard work.

Her father often objected to this; it allowed her so little leisure for numerous important duties, among them those pertaining to a missionary band that was supporting a child in China.

That child in China had a legitimate claim on his daughter's time and interest.

"The greatest fault of our public schools is this everlasting crowding. Why don't these educators see that a few things well done are better than something of this and something of that and something of the other, and this constant crowding to get them."

He always met with concurrent opinion when he made this criticism. It was a very common idea among the parents that their children were over-worked in the high school.

It must appear in exactly this light to those who see only the effort their children make, and know nothing of the results accomplished.

When these same pupils have left the high school and have entered college, they have found the work required of them much more severe. It has required of them at least a year of hard work before they have found themselves capable of grasping readily what is there demanded, or even memorizing with ease.

But that was not the fault of the high school. It had required far less work of them than the schools of Europe require of pupils of the same age.

The cause of this immaturity of grasping power is in the imperfect preparation for doing this work. The method of impressing facts upon the mind so as to call for the least possible effort on the part of the learner is pursued from the chart class to the high school, until when the time comes that the large area to be covered renders this impracticable, and the responsibility is thrown upon the pupil instead of upon the teacher, the effort in accomplishment appears out of all proportion to the results secured.

This effort to make school work captivating, and this disposition to judge a teacher's success by his ability to attract pupils to the school, is disastrous to the best mental development of the child. It takes the dignity out of the work for the pupil. The desirability of education diminishes in the estimation of the child. When he reaches the high school, he considers the few dollars that he can get for a "job" of more value than the high school education. More hard work in the under grades and less "grandmother" discipline would swell our graduating classes.

When those children have left the school and have become the reading public and the listening public, the writer and the speaker must still continue to "entertain," to provide the "bright" and "unique" and cover over their instruction with the same grade of sugar coating that the school teacher used to smear over the morsels of knowledge.

But the girls, as a rule, do not drop out of school at so early an age. Have they more regard for the results of education? Possibly so. Girls are more susceptible to all elevating influences. But there are two other more potent causes.

One of them is that the paying "job" for

the young girl is not so easily obtained. The other is that it is considered quite the thing for the girls to have a career. To insure this she must go on with her education.

In this connection here is another fact.

We are giving so much attention to the preparation of girls for some work outside the home that we are losing sight of the fact that after all the very large proportion of girls will be home-makers and mothers.

It is desirable that the home-making be a matter of choice and not of necessity, and the girls be given the opportunity of preparation to become bread winners for themselves; yet after all the majority of the girls will prefer to become home-makers and mothers, and in the preparation for bread-winners the mother-girl is being neglected.

There is no reason why the girl should not be educated for either vocation. The education of the business girl ought not to interfere with the development of the mother-girl.

But one thing is patent over and above all; the girl who is to be a mother must have good health; education if possible, but health first and education afterwards.

When the education of the girls is arranged so as to insure health, the girl who may not be the home-maker will be just as fortunate in receiving it as the mother-girl.

Once more the wheels of the conference machinery moved, and with this change of the Weaver family Ruth entered the high school where her education was to be finished.

Happy would it have been for her if she, like Dodd, had come in contact with one teacher who understood what the girl needed, and had been possessed of the faculty and the tact to have shown her in true light the narrow, false and selfish life into which she had grown. But this was not to be.

The woman who had charge of this school had come to the position from the humblest walks of life, and to wealth and beauty she still accorded an adoration that she had conceived for them when a little child.

Ruth was immediately classified as "stuck up" by a large portion of the girls, but to the teacher she seemed very charming.

She once more found play for the many little arts that she had formerly employed with such success in the case of former teachers. Before the first week was over she was once more one of the "teacher's pets."

The "pets" were composed of that set of girls whom Ruth would have told you were "toney."

This teacher had never been able in the least degree to associate with this class of girls when she attended school, and in spite of herself she still retained for them something of that feeling that they had then inspired.

The most faithful of her pupils were not the ones who received the greatest share of attention and favor.

She had been ground through the public

school mill; she had been properly clipped
and repressed and moulded and expanded
until she was really a model scholar. When
she graduated she had a thin studious look,
and the glasses that she had been compelled
to wear for four years added to the general
valedictorian air that distinguished her. She
expected to earn her own living and that of
her mother by teaching, and she had kept
that point in view all through her school
career.

She had never been pretty. A round
dimple in her chin had been the only attractive feature of her face, but that had
proved to be an everlasting nuisance inasmuch as it became a convenient receptacle
for crayon dust, and only served to heighten
the school-ma'am effect that had begun to
attach to her before the sleeves of her graduating dress were out of style.

When she had taken her place on the platform to give the valedictory address, the
nerves of her hands seemed to have rebelled
against all control of the will, and her back

gave premonitory symptoms of the same condition of general nervous collapse. It was not due to timorousness for her courage was steel braced.

For days she had been dizzy, weak and nauseated, but she merely called it "tired out." She had no idea what caused this state of nervous distraction. She had learned something of all the sciences, but she was ignorant of the conditions of her own anatomy. So ignorant indeed that she never suspected that her condition was a "tired out" from which she would never become rested.

She had thought that the vacation rest would relieve her aching back, and when in the fall she went to a co-educational college to finish her preparation for teaching, she was discouraged to find the old aches and pains returning at the very first serious exertion.

She had remained three years at this college, where there was less attention given, if such a thing were possible, to girls and their needs than there had been in the public schools.

Three years more of student work, hampered by a malady whose cruelest quality is that it never kills.

Who can measure, or who can know the amount of heroism that thousands of girls are showing in their persistent struggle with this suffering as they drag through their college course.

From the college she had gone to the high school as teacher.

Compelled at last to get medical advice, she began to study into the cause of her suffering. Then she became aware that it had begun away back in the high school, where she had always been compelled to stop at the top of the long stairs from sheer exhaustion.

The teacher of physical culture at the college had always insisted that climbing stairs is really a benefit, if rightly done. She was very positive that, in her case, it had never been "rightly done."

It had been done just as it had been done by the other girls, and as it is done by an infinitely large proportion of humanity, and she was aware that she had suffered from it.

She began to see other causes that accounted for her condition.

She remembered her ignorance, and consequent carelessness. No one had told her what it might mean. Her mother herself did not know. The doctor did not tell her, because she never asked.

She was a conscientious woman. She wanted to do what was right for these girls in her care. What should she do?

She decided that she would begin with a talk with reference to climbing the stairs, and try to impress upon the girls the necessity of care. Accordingly she detained them one afternoon, and standing on the platform before them she began by saying:

"I want to talk to the young ladies in regard to a subject that I think it very important for them to understand. It is in regard to the manner of going up and down stairs."

She went on and tried by the use of general terms to impress upon them her meaning. She had intended to talk very plainly to them, but she found that when she stood before the girls it was no easy matter to say what she wished.

She had not realized the difficulties of her undertaking, but she knew by the look of indifference on their faces and their listless attitudes that the subject had not appealed to them as being of any more importance than a hundred others that she had talked to them about, and she realized as they filed out that she had not made enough of an impression on their minds to have any good result.

Had she heard the scattering remarks in the cloak room, she would have been convinced that her fears were not groundless.

The saucy spirites called to one another.

"What's the matter with the old lady?"

"O, she's got an extra dose of back-ache."

"Look out there, Min! You want to go a little slow down those stairs or something will get you."

"Look at me, girls, look! I'll show you how to go down."

Shrieks of laughter floated into the school room.

Why had she failed? That was one of the problems on which she studied long.

She found that her own impressions of everything associated with sex were so saturated with the moral element that it was impossible to discuss the matter in a philosophical manner. In talking to young ladies she was in constant terror of saying something indelicate.

She tried not to allow this feeling to influence her. She struggled against it in repeated efforts to talk to the girls, but the horrified expression on their faces when she used any term to express her meaning that was out of the vocabulary of common conversation discouraged her.

Gradually she relinquished her efforts,

and silenced her conscience with the argument that she was not responsible for the instruction of these girls in such matters.

She was no doubt right. But the difficulty in doing anything to help the mothers was caused by the utter neglect of the mothers themselves to properly instruct their own girls.

A very large proportion of the girls in that room had received all their knowledge by back door confidences from older girls.

Their very first, and in fact their every impression, was associated with the most vulgar ideas, and it was shocking to hear matters in any way related to these publicly discussed by the teacher.

Information given in a straightforward way when they first began to comprehend these matters would have surrounded the whole subject with a very different atmosphere.

Howbeit, the mothers who intend doing this for their children must needs begin early, or they will find the matter taken out of their hands by enterprising schoolmates, before the children have been in school a term.

By the time that another generation has passed away, if we do not look well to conditions, our school children will have arrived at the same condition as that described of the French children by a plain-spoken author, they will be taught that "It is manly to be nasty," and the morals of the whole nation will be permeated with the same element.

The freedom of the Germans in these things is somewhat shocking to American ears, but it is far better to treat them philosophically than to vilify them after the American fashion.

The teacher who would really benefit the girls under her care, could do no grander work than to send them out with a pure and noble conception of their own creation and destiny.

Convince them that the mission of motherhood is grand; that missing it, they have missed woman's choicest blessing.

But the woman who would do this must be brave as a warrior, for she will find not only that the girls are shocked, but the mothers also.

In this, as in all school reforms, the reformation must begin with the parents. But when it is certain that the children of America are receiving their instruction in regard to the creative power in nature largely in the public schools, and that it is given in the most pernicious manner, cloyed with the most vulgar association and suggestion, how can the conscientious teacher avoid feeling some responsibility for the results?

Ruth's teacher did not have the spirit of a pioneer. She found the enemy within as well as without, and she gave up the battle.

Then when she saw girls like Ruth, foolish, careless, ignorant, she wondered at her own cowardice.

Ruth was now using each day every particle of vitality in her effort to supply all the demands upon her time and strength. She did not deny herself any of the social pleasures of which she was so fond, and she found enjoyment in trying her coquettish arts on the young men.

Almost before she was aware of it came the graduating essay and the graduating dress. She had her customary struggle over the dress.

One thing was certain at the outset; she could never mount that platform, unless her dress was just as good as that of the other girls. "The other girls" meant a few of her companions whose fathers' pockets were very much deeper than Elder Weaver's.

Her persistence had the usual result, and the dress that the pretty daughter of the preacher wore was bought at the sacrifice of the common necessities by the other members of the family.

Ruth had taken for the subject of her graduating essay, "The Lessons of Life." It was not that she had been pondering long upon this subject of life's problems; she selected it because it gave an impression of profundity, for she was determined to have nothing childish for her subject.

She was not the only one of the class who had decided to instruct the audience on subjects that they were much better prepared to speak on than were the writers.

One of the boys would enlighten them on "Can an Honest Man Be a Lawyer?" another would tell about "Our Star of Destiny;" and other similar subjects that would have sent an ordinary divine into a brown study adorned the program.

When Ruth had selected her subject, she wrote it nicely at the top of a clean sheet of paper, and then looked at it for a long time, meditatively chewing her pencil. Finally it began to dawn upon her that she knew nothing about it; but that was no obstacle; she had written a great many essays upon subjects about which she knew nothing. The first and greatest thing was to make a start. She would write something first about the "lessons" in school; then she would go on to the "life" part.   It went very smoothly for a while; she knew something about that, and when she wrote about what she knew, she did very well.

However, the struggle over that essay had just begun, and when it was at last finished, it bristled all over with wise sayings in search of which she had ransacked volumes of essays and sermons.

The audience listened with indulgent patience.   It is astonishing what people will endure when their own children are participants in the program.

There was one grievous disappointment to Ruth, and that was that she must see her name on the elegant, satin-beribboned program just plain Ruth Weaver.   If it could have only been Alice, or May, or Mamie, so that she could have had it printed"Alys" or "Mayme" it would have had so much more "tone."   Even if it had been a middle name it would have answered nicely.   "Miss R. Alys Weaver" would have been quite the thing. But the absence of the unique and picturesque in just "Ruth" was a reflection on that artistic program.

When commencement was over and Ruth's school days were ended, she was exultant. Now would come the promised year with Auntie May. The little wardrobe was gathered together, and she gave a parting kiss to the flock of brothers and sisters, and with a light heart passed out from the minister's home. She would never come again except for very short visits, and it brought a feeling of sadness to the mother's heart as she saw her daughter's glad eagerness to go. It would have been a comfort to have seen a tear for this parting from home and mother; but Ruth had been accustomed all her young life to consider herself alone, and the mother, who had always sacrificed her own comfort for the daughter, found that the daughter valued her very lightly, and the home that had been used merely for her indulgence, and had never claimed anything from her, must expect no affectionate grief at her departure.

She was now a full-fledged young lady, and Auntie May's home was to be the scene of her future career as a maiden. This luxurious home of Mrs. Nelson's had been the fairy-land of her childhood. She had . longed for years to leave the humble parsonage.

Auntie May had lost her little ones when they were infants, and would gladly have opened her heart and home to her brother's child.

"How I would like to take that child! Wouldn't I dress her though!" She had made this remark in Ruth's presence, little realizing what encouragement it gave to her discontent.

"No, May, you can't have her. Our home is full, but there is not one too many."

"You will come when you are through school and stay a year, won't you Ruth?"

And the little girl never forgot her promise.

Now Auntie May was a woman devoted to society and style. She had in her husband a sympathetic companion, whose love of display was almost equal to her own. Their home was the scene of constant gayety, and this life appealed very strongly to Ruth.

Since her marriage Mrs. Nelson had never known what economy meant, and her gifts to the girl had gone far towards enabling her to maintain a proper standing amongst her associates.

This condition of things, however, was now sadly altered, and in the business depression that had ruined so many around him, Mr. Nelson had been barely able to maintain a show of their former style of living. The relations between himself and wife were not as pleasant as they were when neither was compelled to restrain the desire for display, and there were frequent scenes over the bills.

All in vain did he explain and entreat, then storm and swear. She thought he was

very disagreeable, and insisted that it was
very unreasonable to expect her to give up
so small a matter as a new style of hat,
when he indulged in the expensive luxury
of smoking.

These storms over the bills did not shock
Ruth in the least. They reminded her of
the battles she had fought at home, and she
wondered if all men were so mean with
their money. Auntie May was certainly
angelic to bear it so calmly.

Now that Ruth had come with her limited
wardrobe, the question was still more
grave, but she would manage somehow.
Who could tell what they might not be able
to do in a year's time for a pretty girl like
Ruth? She had every marriageable man in
town summed up and ticketed. As soon as
Ruth came she began a rehearsal of the different possibilities, and together they
planned their campaign.

Ruth felt no reluctance in laying her
heart open to Auntie May, for she felt no
fear of her criticisms.

That Ruth could discuss marriage with such sang froid, at first rather startled Mrs. Nelson but finally amused her. She introduced her neice into the young society of the town, and she immediately became a great favorite with the gentlemen.

From their catalogue of possibilities they selected Robert Douglas, who was to be the victim of the first campaign. He was a man of thirty odd years, and a lawyer of marked success. He had inherited considerable wealth, and had bright prospects for enlarging his fortune. He was an educated and cultured man, and they considered him in every way a most desirable match.

"Don't you think that you had better join the Browning club, Ruth? His sister is the president, and they are very literary people. It will never do not to be literary to begin with."

"O, I suppose so; I don't want to in the least. I thought I was through with all that horrid stuff when I left school, and that we were just to have a good time now. But of course I must be literary."

"I know, dear, it's something of a bore, but it would never do not to be literary a little. We won't have to go every week. I only go occasionally myself."

"You will have to go oftener now, Auntie, and tell them I enjoy it so much that I fairly drag you there."

"Ruth, you promise to out-general me."

It was at Mrs. Nelson's home that the enemy's strongholds were first attacked. A new gown was procured for the occasion, and hours were spent at the piano in preparation for the first appearance.

It was not until after the guests had arrived that Mr. Nelson understood their little game, as he called it. He smiled in a cynical way as he soliloquized:

"Now Douglas is no fool. He won't bite. May will find her little game won't work with him."

Mrs. Nelson herself had some fears for the success of her long cherished plans. In

the first place she had some apprehension
lest Ruth might be attracted by some of the
gayer, younger men, and let some silly preference stand in the way of her own best
good; or lest she might not exert herself
to her best efforts; or possibly lest she
might not understand just the proper
way to do it. Her fears were all
in vain. There was no more danger of Ruth
Weaver suddenly finding that her heart had
rebelled against her judgment and was lead-
ing her to sacrifice her worldly interests to
the joys of love, than there was of her so-
phisticated Auntie May advising it; nor
was there any danger of her not knowing
all about the different methods. She had
studied them too long and diligently to be
found wanting at such a critical time.

She knew the exact sweep of the eye-lash
that was the most effective; she knew just
when to dimple her cheeks, and just when
to smile; she had tested these little arts
when she still wore short dresses, and vied

with the other girls for attention from the schoolboys.

She had, moreover, the art of arts; she could employ every one of these seemingly girlish ways with a perfect knowledge of their effect, and yet impress the man with whom she talked with the idea that they were all the unconscious expressions of maiden modesty and sweetness. Even Mr. Nelson thought her a sweet little thing whom it would be a great pity for May to spoil.

Another of Auntie May's fears was lest Mr. Douglas, who was known to be not over sensitive to feminine charms, might not be as responsive as she hoped. Well, they would try him first. If that did not succeed, she would know better how to proceed next time.

It was after supper when Mr. Nelson came into the parlor. He stopped short and looked at the scene at the end of the piano.

Ruth was leaning on her arms, with her

clasped hands reached above her head to the top of the piano. She was looking down, smiling and talking the merest nothings with girlish effervescence. Opposite her stood the lawyer, with a look of admiration on his face that he had never seen there before.

"If Douglas hasn't bit! I'll be ——!" and the rest of the sentence was better smothered before his guests.

After the company had departed, Mrs. Nelson and Ruth sat a long time talking it over. Their verdict was that it was a great success. Ruth repeated everything that would be at all indicative of the impression that she had made, and asked if that pose that she had taken at the end of the piano was not effective.

"Immensely," her auntie assured her. "You must have given that some practice, Ruth."

"O, yes, I have. I consider that one of my best."

"Well, how do you like him? He is fine, I think."

"O, he is all right."

Ruth had been so engaged making an impression herself, that she really had not thought much about the man.

"O, but I am so tired, Auntie! It seems as if I could scarcely walk up stairs."

"Well, don't come down in the morning until you please. We will have to get around in time for Mrs. Wilson's luncheon, but there is no need for you to get up before noon."

"I don't know as that will make much difference, for I am just awfully tired all the time. I thought that when I came here I should certainly get rested, but I don't."

"O, well, you must get used to that. Women are always more or less tired unless they are very common. If you continue to succeed as well as you did to-night with Mr. Douglas, you will have nothing to do but rest."

If Mr. Nelson was astonished at the ease

with which his wife and niece captured the
lawyer, he was still more so that he continued to show the same interest.

He remarked to his wife.

"That gets me, that a man like Douglas
will run around after a chit of a girl like
Ruth, and let you folks work him in that
style. Why, he's one of the shrewdest law-
yers around here, and I've known him to
see through schemes at the caucuses when
the rest of us fellows were blind as bats.
Now he's letting himself be made a fool of
by a couple of women."

"I don't see the use, Richard, in your
talking in that way. Why do you call a
man a fool, simply because he likes a pretty
girl? Ruth is certainly very charming, and
Mr. Douglas may consider himself fortunate if he gets such a lovely wife. I'm not
at all certain that Ruth would have him."

A significant grunt was all the rejoinder
that Mr. Nelson made as he sipped his cof-
fee. They were alone at the breakfast table,

as Ruth seldom came down in time for the morning meal.

It did certainly appear that Mr. Nelson's prophecy that his friend would fall an easy prey to the wiles of his wife and niece would be fulfilled.

All through the summer months Ruth was devoting her entire energy to the cause. The mornings were spent in bed, or in discussing the next new costume, or in complaining attempts to prepare for the next meeting of the Browning Club.

"Do you know, Auntie, Mr. Douglas asked me what I thought of Browning's poem on "The Book," and if I didn't think that passage about Art speaking truth obliquely, or some such thing, was particularly fine. I declare, Auntie, I was perfectly rattled for a minute. I didn't know what to answer. I didn't just want to confess that I had never read it when he thinks that I have been in absorbing study of Browning ever since I have been here."

"Well, what did you say?"

"O, I said 'Do explain that to me. I have often wondered just what Browning meant by that. He is so obscure.' So he explained it all to me in the most obliging way. I must read it now so that I can quote a line or two some day and tell him it is so beautiful since he explained it to me."

"Ruth, you are cute. What a true disciple to the new idea you are! I was a great deal older than you before I discovered that wise men do love a woman that they can explain things to."

"I never pretend to know anything for real sure with him, and he is just lovely about explaining things. In fact, Auntie May, I don't know what we should talk about some of the time, if I didn't keep a lot of things on hand to be explained. When I get short I always ask something about law and that keeps him going quite a while."

"That will all do very well for a starter, Ruth, but we must do something to bring matters to a crisis. He has been coming here for three months, and things seem no nearer to an understanding than before."

"O, I can soon manage that when the proper time comes. We are going driving to-morrow night, and it will be lovely moonlight."

"I see I can trust you, Ruth. I thought you would need some pointers. I have been picking them up for years, and have been in society constantly, but, I declare, you can give them to me. Where did you learn all this?"

"O, in school."

"In school? What do you mean?"

"O, we used to tell each other how we worked those things on the boys, and we got the benefit of one another's experience. There are a variety of ways. It all depends on the boy and the time, Auntie."

"Well, I declare, you girls are too wise for your age. You certainly belong to a different generation from what I did. I see you are fully capable of taking care of yourself."

There was consternation in the camp at

Auntie May's when Ruth received a note
from Mr. Douglas saying that his mother's
sudden illness had made it necessary for
him to accompany her to Chicago, and he
feared that he might not be able to return
for some time.

"How disgusting!" exclaimed Ruth. "If
I had known that I could just as well have
had everything arranged before he went."

There was nothing to do but to accept
the inevitable; and when a letter came later
from Mr. Douglas Ruth complained bitterly
at her fate in being compelled to write.
When she had curls and blue eyes and
smiles at her command she could manage
him all right, but a page of paper remote
from herself was a different thing.

Her writing since she had left school had
consisted almost entirely of a few very short
letters to her mother, and some more
lengthy ones to the girls at home. Mr.
Douglas figured largely in these. She had
to rely chiefly on Auntie May's devices for
filling out a page, and when Mr. Douglas,

instead of returning in the winter months, had taken his mother to Florida, her disgust knew no bounds.

"I had planned everything to have the wedding at the Holidays, and now he says that he don't know when he can return. His mother must be very childish to want him with her all the time."

"They say she is very weak, and he was always devoted to her."

"Well, there is nothing to be done but to have a good time until he does come back, I suppose."

"I don't know, Ruth; I am really afraid that we shall have to do something. Richard told me last night that they had lost considerable by that last failure, and that money would be exceedingly scarce. I do wish it was as it used to be, and that I could do for you everything that I want to, but really I can not see how we are going to manage about your new wrap and winter clothing. You couldn't get work in the school at your home, could you?

But of course you must be here when Mr. Douglas comes back. It would be rank folly not to follow that up. O, I have an idea! Milly Sanders is not going to be able to teach after Christmas, and I believe we could get that school for you."

"O, Auntie May! How ever can I? I don't know as I can get a certificate."

"Why, you certainly can, Ruth. You were always considered a good scholar, and it will not be for long, you know. He will certainly be back by the Holidays. Richard said that he had an important case coming on in the January term of court, and he will have to be here, and it may be that you will not have to teach more than a term. I am dreadfully sorry, Ruth, but I know there is no use asking Richard for anything more. You know that he is really so liberal when he does have money. You might just as well give up the battle at once, if you can not have a proper wardrobe. You can board with us, and I can help you some. You know you will need so many things. I am sure that Richard can get the place for you."

Ruth finally decided to make the attempt. When Uncle Richard was approached, he was very willing to try what he could do for her.

"If it isn't promised already, I know I can get the place for you, for I have a pull with several of those fellows on the school board." The place was not promised, and Mr. Nelson employed his "pull" with good effect. Thus it came about that at the beginning of the winter term Ruth found herself in the school room again.

Some wondered at her election, for she had had no "experience" nor special preparation, and there were girls of their own town and school much better prepared for the work.

When the members of the school board were asked about it, no one seemed to know anything about the circumstances; in reality they knew exactly how it happened. They did not feel free to confess this knowledge, nor to expose the members who had been influential in the matter. There was no knowing how soon they might want a like favor themselves. They felt no personal responsibility.

Conscience is so much more callous, collectively, than it is individually.

When Ruth first stepped into the room where she was to preside as teacher, there was rank rebellion in her heart. How dreadful that she must do this just because she must have a new wrap this winter. Auntie May said it would cost fifty dollars to get what she really ought to have. She would have to teach more than a month to earn that. Why couldn't her father have sent her that much money? It was decidedly mean of him. Uncle Richard was a regular miser, too; and if Mr. Douglas' inconsiderate old mother hadn't gotten sick just at the wrong time she could have been in Florida herself now, instead of being shut up with those hateful children. It was by a very great effort that she kept back the tears, while the children in the room were all watching her face, trying to decipher their probable fate for the coming term.

Ruth's forebodings of her abhorrence of her work were more than justified before many weeks had gone by. Every night she returned from her work with aching back and tingling nerves. Pandemonium reigned in the school room. She heartily hated every one of the little animals that tortured her, and they reciprocated the feeling with a manifest energy that did credit to the age that has been called the animal age of childhood.

The friends of the other candidates pointed with great satisfaction to her failure, and hoped to see the position soon vacant again.

When Ruth drew her first month's pay, it did not seem possible to her that all those days of misery should have been necessary to produce just one fur cape.

"Auntie, I won't have to spend it all for just a cape, will I?"

"Why, certainly, dear; that will not be

much to put in a wrap. You can't begin to
get anything that will answer for less."

This was said in the presence of Uncle
Richard.

"Learning the value of a dollar, hey?
Didn't know they came so high."

Ruth thought that was brutal, but Uncle
Richard really looked at it in the light of a
favor to his friend Douglas.

"I wish some one had taught May what a
dollar costs before she was married. She
hasn't the least conception."

At last the time was at hand for Mr.
Douglas' return. Then one noon Mr. Nelson announced that the mother had died
and that they were bringing her home for
burial.

"Now, that is too bad," said Auntie May.

The expression sounded very sympathetic, but the sympathy was for Ruth. She
foresaw in this another obstacle to their
plans.

Mr. Douglas was home for several weeks
before he called again. The Nelson home

did not have as much attraction for him as before his departure, for the insipidity of Ruth's letters had banished many of the impressions left by her bright smiles.

"Now, Auntie, you must help me out. I don't want Mr. Douglas to have any idea why I went to teaching. You must give him the right impression. I saw him today, and he is going to call tonight."

Auntie May needed no instructions to do the right thing in this regard.

Ruth was in her room when he was ushered into the parlor that evening, and Auntie May thought this a good opportunity to make a few remarks that she had prepared.

"Ruth is resting," she said, "but I will call her."

"O, do not disturb her if she is resting."

"She would never forgive me if I did not. She gets very tired teaching. She has such an independent nature that she simply would not consent to let us do what we wanted to for her. She insisted on teaching, and it is a terrible tax on her strength. She throws her whole soul into the work, and I think that it is too much for a frail girl like her to be shut up with all those children. I can not persuade her to give it up. But I will call her. You must never let her know what I have said."

In a few moments Ruth appeared, and Mr. Douglas was impressed with the truth of these remarks, when he saw how very listless and worn she was. But this did not last long; in a few moments the old animation returned. Lassitude may do very well to create sympathy, but it soon grows wearisome. When Mr. Douglas was leaving, Auntie May came into the hall and, throwing her arms around Ruth's shoulders, said:

"You must come often, Mr. Douglas, and cheer up our girlie. She gives so much of her vitality to that school that she is really depriving herself of society. I don't know when I have seen her enjoy herself as she has tonight."

Mr. Douglas assured them that he would be delighted to come often.

"Well, that was a good evening's work, Ruth; I feel as if we had the thing started again." This was Auntie May's good-night remark.

The promise to come often was fulfilled, and inasmuch as Ruth insisted that, being absorbed in her work, she really cared nothing for society, he found a growing attraction in the Nelson home.

Ruth realized what it might mean to fail in her plans, and her ardor in the undertaking was renewed.

"Now, Ruth, you must not let this go on any longer. You must bring things to a focus at once. There is no telling what may happen. His sister may get sick next. It really frightened me the way things looked for a while."

"Well, I was just going to suggest that you go away, Auntie. I shall have to have him alone, you know."

"I will go off for a week, dear, and give you the best of chances."

So Auntie May informed Mr. Douglas that she would leave Ruth for a week, and she hoped that he would see that she did not suffer from loneliness.

The first evening that he called, Ruth had her plans all laid. The daintiest of costumes and the sweetest of smiles were prepared, and the delighted way in which she came forward and gave him her hand, saying that she was just perishing from loneliness, and that it was just lovely of him to come, quite charmed him.

She gave him a seat opposite her, over in front of the grate; then she leaned forward in a most bewitching way, with the light reflecting from the large pink lamp shade upon her fair head.

After a few moments the conversation turned upon some of the new actresses that were appearing, and Ruth went to bring a magazine that contained some of their pictures. She sat down on a low stool beside him and opened the book.

"Isn't that the loveliest face? I just envy her," she said, as she opened the book to the photogravures. "I just envy her, she is so sweet."

Mr. Douglas could never have given a lucid account of what followed, but Ruth could have told you just what came next through each of the successive steps by which she led this astute lawyer.

It was long after his usual hour when he left the Nelson home that night, and he was really a little surprised when he considered that the sweet little creature that he had left behind was his promised wife. He actually could not tell just how it all happened, but he certainly was glad that it had happened.

"Well, what success?" was Auntie May's first question on her return.

"O, he came beautifully, Auntie. It was all done the very first evening. He's ever so much easier than those horrid young fellows that act as if they were doing you a favor."

Ruth, however, had not accomplished all of her plans. She wanted to convince Mr. Douglas of the desirability of having the wedding in March, as that would allow her to resign her position in the school. She had an uncomfortable apprehension that the school board might accomplish her release in a less graceful manner, although her uncle assured her that he would see to it that she held the position as long as she chose.

She could not tell Mr. Douglas the truth, for Auntie May had repeatedly dwelt upon her devotion to her work. Accordingly, she laid the matter before her.

"He does not seem to think that there is any possibility of such a thing, and I can't make him see any necessity of it. I really believe that he does not seriously consider our having the wedding before next fall."

"O, we must have it at least by June, Ruth. I'll try what I can do."

But even Auntie May's clever strategies

failed of their purpose, and Ruth closed her winter term of school with anticipations of another three months of misery.

The criticisms on her work had been so emphatic that the board talked the matter over in a formal way; but as the member who had secured her election insisted that she be retained there was nothing done about it, and the helpless children were doomed to another term under this teacher, whose nerves were so racked that every movement of theirs tortured her. It would have been a greater kindness in the board to have paid her dry goods bill and let them revel in the sunshine in the park.

But even a school term will come to an end, and at last Ruth was free. The hours in the school room were not the only ones that were a tax on her strength. The question of what to do to entertain her future husband in his frequent calls was one of vital importance.

There is no need of preparation for a pair of bona fide lovers, but the affection in this

case was so entirely on one side that even
reasonably responsive submission to his
caresses soon grew wearisome to her, and
she preferred to lead him on in conversation
on subjects where he could instruct and she
could listen.

"What shall we talk about tonight,
Auntie? Can't you give me a leader?"

"Get Richard's North American Review.
There is an article on George Eliot in it.
You know something about that subject.
Get some questions ready."

"How can I ever stand this, Auntie, when
I am married? I won't have you to help
me, and I shall surely perish."

"O, no you won't. He will go down town
evenings in a very short time. You know
there is a honeymoon for just such men as
he is, and when that wanes you will find that
he will not trouble you much. Richard
goes away almost every night now, although he used to stay at home a great deal
when we were first married. I think from
what I know of you that you can be trusted

to manage all those small points when once you are married. I am sure you have done beautifully so far. It is a perfect marvel to me where you learned all those things."

"I am sure I can't tell you, Auntie. It seems as if I always knew them. Why, I heard the older girls tell about them when I was in the primary, and we used to think it was great fun to practice them when we were older."

"Well, there is one thing certain. No woman is likely to be imposed on when she knows as much as you do. But we must try some way to get that wedding settled for June. June weddings are lovely, although I suppose that he will be scandalized at the idea of the wedding so soon after his mother's death."

"Then you must help me. Just tell him that I shall go away as soon as school is out if we are not married."

On the first occasion Auntie May told Mr. Douglas that she was utterly unhappy at the thought of spending the summer alone. She had become so much accustomed to dear Ruth's society, and now her mother insisted on her coming home as soon as school was over.

"I don't know, but I shall have to appeal to you, Mr. Douglas, to help me out. I am sure the summer without her will be dreadful."

"Now, Auntie, you are making a great mistake. Men are not so dependent upon the mere joys of society as we giddy women are. You don't suppose that Robert is going to pine for me this summer."

And she gave such a sweet little laugh, and looked up with such a bewitching air, that Robert was tempted to kiss her instanter, regardless of all company. He insisted instead that he would miss her immensely, and that he must devise some plans for keeping her.

With some further suggestions from Auntie May, it was finally decided that the marriage should occur in a very quiet manner in June.

"I don't see why this could not have been settled before just as well. We will have to hurry abominably now," Auntie May remarked, as soon as they were alone.

And now began the usual preparation that is thought necessary for a girl who is about to be married. Every possibility of obtaining the necessary dollars was canvassed, but it was evident that there was going to be a painful shortage.

As soon as the school house door was closed behind Ruth at night she was plunged into the excitement of shopping and dress-making.

But the bills mounted up in a most shocking manner. She could not reconcile the difference between the value of a ten-dollar bill as represented by the amount of labor it required from her to earn it, and the amount of merchandise she was able to procure with it.

"What shall I do, Auntie? I haven't paid for that mull and organdie yet. I haven't but two pairs of shoes, and you thought I ought at least to have four, and it will take every cent I can hope for from the school to pay the dressmaker and milliner. There will be at least fifty dollars at the dry goods store besides."

"Well, cheer up, dear. Just remember this is your last struggle. But you can not do without a single one of those dresses. It would be ruinous for you to get married with a shabby trousseau. Now, when you need anything hereafter you won't have to consider each penny so closely."

"Well, that don't dispose of the present troubles. There is no doubt that I need every one of those things. I will have them, and I do wish that I had a little of that here-after money on hand. O, I have an idea, Auntie. Why wouldn't this be just the scheme? Can't you have them charge that dry goods bill to you, and then hold them off until I can pay you?"

It was considered a very brilliant idea, and an extra dress was added to the list immediately. Each day was crowded full of excitement and work, until at last the long-desired June came, and only the final preparations remained.

Ruth longed for an elaborate affair, with a bower of roses and a table full of presents, but it was one of the points that Mr. Douglas had insisted upon, that out of respect to his mother it be a very quiet affair.

"Do not bring but two of the children," Ruth wrote to her mother. "Of course, papa will have to be here if possible, or else Uncle Richard will have to give me away."

Ruth was very much pleased that the ceremony was to be one in which the giving away of the bride would be necessary. This relic of feudal ideas appealed to her. She looked upon it as a matter of course that she must be the property of some man, and that in being transferred to a husband she must be formally bestowed by the former proprietor. She cared nothing for that liberty that would make her an individual capable of governing herself. She much pre-

ferred throwing the responsibility upon
some one else.

The wedding day came at last, a beautiful
June day that a bride might consider perfect. The sun shone gloriously, and if there
was to be any truth in the old adage, "Happy is the bride that the sun shines on," Ruth
was to be radiantly happy, for it sent a
shower of golden shafts on her young head.

To the little company gathered in Mrs.
Nelson's parlor it seemed that there was
every prospect of a blissful journey through
life for the sweet bride and manly bridegroom.

There were a few suspicious ones, however. The bridegroom's sister, Irene, who
idolized her brother, and who had monop-
olized his attention for so many years, did
not feel altogether kindly toward the young
girl who had so successfully transferred his
affections to herself. The real Ruth who ex-
isted under the smiling exterior was well
understood by her.

Early in her brother's courtship, when she

saw whither things were tending, she had ventured to criticise Ruth to him.

"O, don't be so hard on her, sis. You women are just merciless with one another."

Her woman's sense told her she was too late, and she had thereafter simply maintained complete silence on the subject. She saw for her brother many things of which the June sunshine never hinted.

Ruth's mother stood sadly watching her daughter as the minister pronounced her the wife of the man beside her. Her thoughts went bounding back to the night when she had stood a proud, hopeful and happy bride. Would this man appreciate the precious charge he had in her beautiful daughter? O, she would have given her heart's blood to have insured happiness to that daughter.

She struggled with her thoughts and her tears until she had given the first kiss to the young wife, then she slipped quietly out of the room, and in the corner of the dark cloak closet the sobs and tears burst beyond her control. She could scarcely have told why, only that a great burden of fear for that dear child seemed to oppress her.

Why is it that mothers always feel this sorrow when they see their daughters enter upon the life of a wife? They look on resignedly enough when their sons are married, but when it is the daughter there seems to be a tugging at the heart strings that sends them hurrying from the presence of the bride, that her joy may not be dampened by the tears.

What do they know that is sealed from their daughters? A doubt came to Ruth's mother then. A feeling that perhaps she had failed in not acquainting her daughter more with the hard, stern facts of the life before her. She knew that she had done just as her mother did, but here was her frail, delicate daughter, worn to the very last shred of strength, fragile in health for years, about to become the wife of a strong, virile man, and never suspecting that the life before her would not be all rosy with sentiment.

Why had she hesitated to tell Ruth the many things that a young wife would be so much wiser to know? Why need the young wife enter the married life with ideas so different from the realities? Why can she not have the same knowledge and the same view of the nature that God has implanted in men that her mother or her husband has? Would it harm her? Would she not be a better and a happier wife if this knowledge could come with the right light that an experienced and loving mother could throw on it? If every mother could throw from between herself and her daughter every vestige of reserve and talk freely, the first year of married life would not be the most critical, and often the most disastrous of all.

But how had this mother come through it? Love, strong, pure love had been the power. Would it prove the same in Ruth? Would a closer knowledge of each other's needs bring them at last to that oneness of feeling that is ideal for man and wife? Perhaps,—if the love was there in all the fullness that the husband believed it to be,—but—, the mother sobbed again.

Auntie May came to the door.

"Now, don't feel bad, Mary. Ruth is doing very nicely, and she will have a lovely home."

"O, I don't doubt that, May; but you know she is very delicate. Perhaps she don't realize——"

"O, she will be all right. She is awfully tired now, but then you know we were just the same way when we were married. We can't expect girls to be at their best at such a time. She has worked constantly for weeks to get ready, besides her school work, but she will have a chance to rest now."

"Yes, I know; but——"

"Well, let us go back to the parlor. She has just what she wanted, and I am sure that we couldn't have done better for her."

When Mrs. Weaver returned to the parlor all was life and vivacity again. The first few impressive moments and the first congratulations, when everything threatens to collapse into utter silence, were happily over, and a brusque uncle of the groom met her at the door.

"Well, I suppose you are like the rest of the mothers; you hate to see your daughter married, and yet you wouldn't have her do otherwise for the world?"

"O, yes, of course we want the girls to get married, but——"

"They are 'white funerals' sure enough, Mrs. Weaver," put in his wife. "Mr. Douglas is always making fun of us women, just because I felt so badly when our Grace was married."

"Well, wife, I see no need to feel badly when a girl marries Rob; he's gold way through."

"It isn't Rob, William. You don't understand."

"All right; I'll admit that you women are great big riddles."

Two hours later the bride and groom had

bidden farewell to their friends, and were leaving for their wedding trip.

It had not been Mr. Douglas' idea to leave on this trip. He much preferred to go at once to their own beautiful home, where his wife would find rest and quiet.

Ruth was so evidently disappointed at this suggestion that he had readily acquiesced in her desire for a wedding trip.

She wished to visit some of the eastern watering places of which she had read so much.

"You will find them the stupidest places in the world, Ruth, unless you go with a party. I think they are great bores. Wouldn't you like to go to the National Park now, or even take a trip to Alaska?"

But nothing would satisfy Ruth except some eastern summer resort. The simple pleasure to be derived from viewing nature's living wonders did not in the least appeal to her.

As she leaned back on the cushions of the parlor car, she felt that every trial of her

14

life was past. At last she had what she desired, and now there was nothing left but
enjoyment. She laid her head back with a
long drawn sigh.

"Are you tired, dearest?"

"Very."

"Let me put your hat in the rack. You
can rest so much better. It is going to be a
long, tiresome ride."

The kind thoughtfulness brought a smile
of appreciation.

She closed her eyes for a moment. Every
nerve was tingling; every muscle was aching; she felt that she would scream if any
one were to speak to her suddenly. Her
hand lay on the arm of the chair. Her husband laid his own tenderly over it.

She gave a start, opened her eyes, and
then drew her hand away.

She was too miserably sick and tired to
endure a caress, much less to respond to it.

A look of surprise came into her husband's face, which was quickly followed by

a flush of mortification and anger. He turned and looked out of the window for a long time without speaking.

And thus she started on her married life.

WOMANHOOD.

"All love that hath not friendship for its base
Is like a mansion built upon the sand."

The honeymoon season was far in the past. Now, when there was any moonlight visible at all in the Douglas household it was shed from a very ordinary moon, exceedingly uninteresting except for the wry faces that it insisted on making, betokening sometimes dry weather and sometimes wet; or quite possibly it was encircled by a ring prophetic of coming storms; or else it sent a lurid light slanting across their vision that told of days to come that were long and hot and dusty.

But that limpid, silvery affair that shone in delicate crescent on the heads of bride and groom was nowhere to be seen.

To the husband that honeymoon season had been shorter far than to the bride. The domestic heavens were soon clouded, and he saw with dismay the bright orb disappear, together with her attendant stars, until now scarcely one was to be seen; certain it was that Venus did not shed her sparkling rays upon them, for she had trailed after the honeymoon in a disgracefully rapid manner.

And now, when the enchantment of moon and stars was gone, and the plain light of day finally shone on him again, he saw with clearer vision just what the other days that were to come might have in store for him.

He was a man of the dispassionate nature that views marriage from the standpoint of common sense. He had always meant to marry some day and rear his family around his hearth, but he was aware that mistakes were common, and he had it well fixed in mind to guard against such failure by careful choice amongst the maidens of his acquaintance.

He had considered the matter well, and could have told you his preference in size, in color, in age, in temperament, and was ready, now that he had passed the folly of youth, to choose this companion of his life.

He had heard much about *choosing* a wife. He would have been loath to admit that he intended to look her over with a view to possession, just as he would before he purchased a horse. He would have been farther yet from doing it. Men rarely *choose* a wife, it is but fair to presume, when we compare the much-chosen ones with those that are left unmolested. Fate is very apt to take men by the nape of the neck and cram some Miss otherwise difficult to dispose of down their throats. Fate has a mighty grip on humanity. No doubt in this way it keeps the balance even through the generations, and in this way prevents the division of human kind into two great classes of fools and wise.

Robert Douglas did not reckon well, if he thought that age would so forestall the foolishness of masculine susceptibility that at thirty he could, with cool and deliberate wisdom, choose a wife. He could do it no better then than at twenty.

Amongst the many homely truths that have been formulated for us by our ancestors, there is none truer than this, "There is no fool like an old fool," unless, alas! we are compelled to amend it to read, "two old fools." Melancholy is the truth that a man's wisdom in choosing a wife seems to be in inverse ratio to his years.

Robert Douglas, in the ordinary affairs of life, was far from that condition in which men do deeds at which their brothers scoff.

If in moments when the burden seemed insufferable he blamed himself for blindness, he need but look around him to know that he was not the first wise man who let his wisdom go to the winds when he was most in need. We look with greater pity on these men, who, blessed with much that is good, yet have something that is not the best in womankind. It may be but a divine dispensation; for while nature and art combine to produce these women, it is best that they be disposed of where they will do the least harm. Let the men who are rich in other blessings take care of them.

While this may be very good and very just as a universal principle, yet to Robert Douglas it was most unsatisfactory.

He wanted his love to have "friendship for its base," and he could not conceive, although two years of his married life had rolled away, why the girl who had seemed so absorbed in a beautiful bit of Browning now turned wearily from any suggestion to read more of the mystic poet. He could not blame himself; the change was in the girl. Certain it was that in the days of the courtship there had been every promise of a beautiful friendship growing up between them; and he had pictured the evenings at the fireside where the sweet young wife would be happy in being led along the paths of beauty where his superior knowledge would render him a fitting guide.

Although his experience had taught him that our ideals are seldom realized, the real-

ity of the long cherished home life appalled
him. His fireside had been to him, as it always is to men of poetic temperaments, a
haven where he retired for rest and enjoyment; but now when his wife was there
their worlds were as far apart as the poles.
She sat absorbed in a story that to him
would be inane, repulsive, or even painful;
or reading with minute care instructions on
"How to keep young"; or studying with intense interest the latest sweep of skirt, or
build of choker.

He was left to dream his dreams, as much
alone as he was before she came; indeed,
more alone; for then he had ideals, now so
evidently false in the face of the hard facts
before him.

The beautiful sentiment in "Locksley
Hall" was ruined for him, for involuntarily
the "Amy" would take on the flower face of
the wife opposite to him, and he would consider Tennyson mighty lucky in his first disappointment.

But not often was he allowed even this

ghost of contentment, for even the novel
and the fashion plate and the instructions
on facial massage soon wearied, and the demand for social pleasures, that were life to
her and hollow mockeries to him, became
so insistent that he yielded, and in the
smoking room at the dancing parties he be-
guiled the weary hours, until his wife, her
powers of endurance exhausted, was ready
to leave the scene of gayety.

She was in her youth. Twelve years her
senior, he found that she could not leap the
intervening time; and had their tastes been
similar instead of diverse, he would have
found that the girl would naturally live out
her girlhood, be she wife or maiden.

At home his own genial hospitality was
turned into a travesty. The hearty welcome that had always been accorded to his
friends at his board and at his fireside, was
turned into scenes of display and frivolity.

Where he had formerly stood the genial
host, he now was his wife's husband, who
did the honors at frequent entertainments

to a flock of butterfly folk, who were invited merely in acknowledgment of social indebtedness.

Ruth found her ideal happiness in this life. She had no complaints to make. Even their honeymoon had not brought to her the startling disappointment that had overwhelmed her husband. She had not expected the same style of a moon. It was unreasonable to expect an ordinary honeymoon to be

"All poetic, romantic and tender;
    Hanging with jewels a cabbage-stump,
    And investing a common post or a pump,
    A currant-bush or a gooseberry clump,
    With a halo of dreamlike splendor."

She had deemed a practical honeymoon that would shed a ray not too oppressive in its sentiment, far preferable.

To reign supreme in one devoted heart soon grew monotonous, and she was glad when the bridal days were past, and she escaped from the too devoted attentions of a loving bridegroom.

He was certainly ideal in his treatment of
her. She had her plans all arranged for a
campaign on the money question, should
her husband prove to have as disagreeable
notions about controlling expenses as did
Auntie May's. She was quite surprised on
their first return to have him tell her that
he would never have his wife take the attitude of a suppliant toward him; that when
he had said, "With my worldly goods I thee
endow," he had not considered it a mere
form. His bank account was as free to her
as to himself.

So the matter of money was forever settled between them.

It was an ideal condition, but, alas! a noble ideal and a wife that is not noble will not
harmonize, and as her aspirations began to
enlarge, and her ambitions to lead in the
social life around her led her on to greater
expenses, he wondered how one woman
could dispose of so much money, and yet
show no results but the gratification of her
own vanity.

Very mildly he tried to give her some idea of the condition of his finances, and hoped that the knowledge of the family income would guide her into reasonable expenditures. After all his explanations she answered:

"I never thought that you would be miserly, but I suppose that all men are."

The old relation between fifty dollars and the labor that represents it that she had learned in the school room seemed to exist no longer. The thought of value was hateful to her, and she continued in her extravagance until her husband was desperate in the necessity of restraining her in her unreasonable expenditures.

The failure of the bank account did not cause her the least concern, and in reply to her husband's persistent appeals for less extravagant expenses she coolly remarked that the getting of money was not her part of the affair; if it were she would see to it that it was provided.

After a while there came a time when her

pleasure-seeking was interrupted, when she saw that her gay life must be forfeited, and that more serious duties were soon to rest upon her, that she made the recollection of his bachelor days appear to her husband like a paradise.

The vain, selfish woman became the complaining, peevish woman, and the wail over her misfortune was so constant that the sister Irene had ample opportunity to demonstrate the point that she had made from the beginning, that Ruth lacked good sense.

But Mr. Douglas could not admit, even to his sister, that his wife had been a disappointment. He was too loyal hearted. It is a sign of the most hopeless condition of conjugal happiness when a man admits to another his wife's shortcomings.

"You must remember that Ruth has never been well," he explained.

It was too true; neither morally nor physically had she known what sound health meant, and he spoke truer than he knew. ·

Nature would have compelled a wholesome woman to respond to the constant affection that had surrounded Ruth through the years of her married life, and would have opened to her a wonderful new beauty in the little life that was coming, compared to which the sacrifice of her mere social pleasures would have been nothing.

That this hope and sweetness failed to come to Ruth in her new condition, made her husband even more solicitous. He had hoped that the new little life would open the true womanly nature of his wife and give that richness that so often comes with motherhood.

It had been a long cherished wish to have a little one in their home, and all the sympathy and gentleness of which he was capable was poured out to his wife. But the fuller the measure the more she demanded, for she felt that she was being imposed upon in the most unreasonable manner, and she was exasperated that she was not able to shift this new responsibility upon some one else. It had rarely occurred to her in her

life that she had been compelled to do disagreeable things against her will. There
had been always some way provided for her
escape; some one else upon whom she
could unload her burden. It was galling to
her pride and her vanity that she was forced
to bear this one entirely alone, and she felt
nothing but bitterness toward the little life
that was the cause of her misfortune.

The little one seemed to have felt the
chill life that was awaiting it, for with one
faint cry it went back again into the vast and
mysterious eternity from whence it came.

The young mother had not vitality
enough to launch another life; yet while
she could not give the little one strength
enough for a start in life, certain it is she
gave it all that she had. The weeks were
prolonged into months before she sat again
at the fireside.

With kindest sympathy her husband tried
to encourage her, but she felt herself to have
been too much abused ever to regard him
again as anything but her persecutor. The

relations between the two, instead of growing closer, only widened.

As soon as sufficient strength returned,
she insisted upon going to Chicago, where
Mr. Nelson had moved his family the year
previous, to stay with Auntie May and be
under the care of a specialist.

And now a new regime began. It was
the reign of the Doctor.

She had hoped for a return of even her
former delicate health, when she should
come under his care; but she was doomed
to bitter disappointment, for only for short
periods did she ever know even the sem-
blance of health. Every interruption of
constant medical care would send her back
to her old condition of weakness.

It was unreasonable to expect the doctors to rebuild her constitution and implant
in her frame the strength and elasticity that
should have been ingrown through years of
culture.

It was not easy to see just where she had
been benefited by the enforced attendance

at school, high grade attendance rolls, close confinement, constant mental drill, and high nervous pressure.

The thrills of pride that her teacher had enjoyed in the display of all this systematic and punctilious work scarcely compensated her for her shattered constitution.

Even the increase in the treasury of the Epworth League, or the constant attendance at all sorts of musical and social affairs seemed matters of small importance now.

Womanhood, uniformly developed, must be the aim of a girl's education.

Motherhood, strong and capable, must be the focal point of her development.

Scorn to the scoffer who would degrade it by ignoring its potency.

Ruth might have been everything of which she was capable, if she had been capable of being a good mother.

She was in reality a sick woman; but she was infinitely worse because it suited the role she played. Unable to engage except in a limited degree in her former festivities, she assumed the part of invalid, and increased her demands for consideration.

She was a martyr, and in compensation the utmost that the household could do seemed inconsiderable. She resented their interest in anything outside of herself, and would not condescend to consider the discussion even of her husband's most vital business interests worthy of listening to, and certainly not deserving of the lively attention that his sister Irene gave them.

The short visits to the city were soon extended, until the time that Robert Douglas' wife was in his home was much shorter than the time that she spent away from it.

At last he was forced to the humiliating acknowledgment that his wife was a failure. Irene answered with emphasis:

"Well, I simply would not endure it."

"What would you do?"

"Well, I would do something."

"Pray, what would it be?"

"I would never have married her."

"Very wise, no doubt; but, unfortunately, a trifle too late."

"I certainly should not live with her."

"I don't very much."

"Well, she should not be my wife."

"Would you have me apply for a divorce?"

"N-n-o-o, you couldn't. She comes home too often for that; but her extravagance is ruining you, and she cares nothing for you."

"I see nothing to do but simply to endure it."

And he did endure it with dignity before all the world, except that one sister.

Even Auntie May could not approve of Ruth, although her home was always open to her.

"A man has some rights, Ruth," she said.

"Well, I have not infringed on any of his rights at all. He never knew me to ask him a question, or criticise a thing that he ever did; and that is more than Uncle Richard can say of you."

"I rather think it is; but then I don't go

away and leave him alone by the month. Your mother doesn't approve of your way of living at all, Ruth."

"O, mama is so old-fashioned! She would have me trailing around with a whole household of babies if she had her way; but I assure you she never will. Why, if I had been tied at home with a baby last week I could not have come in when I heard that Irving and Terry were going to be here; besides, you know, I have to keep near my doctor."

Mr. Nelson came in in time to hear the last of her remarks.

"The doctor! I get so infernally tired of hearing about the doctor and sick women that I wish the whole tribe would perish."

"That's rather strong, Richard, it appears to me. Which tribe do you refer to? The women, or the doctors?"

"I meant the doctors. But I should say, from all the complaining women I hear, that they were in a fair way to perish if they were just left alone."

"Well, Richard, we can't help being sick. You don't suppose we are so just for the pure pleasure that there is in it, do you?"

"Don't ask me for the reason. I give it up."

Mrs. Nelson gave it up, too. Ruth never made any effort to study into causes. She knew that she was sick, and that was enough. But that she was mentally and morally, as well as physically diseased, no one but the neglected husband at home fully realized.

www.ingramcontent.com/pod-product-compliance
Lightning Source LLC
Chambersburg PA
CBHW022001050726
47498CB00007BA/2353